FERDINAND OYONO was born in 1929 in Cameroon, and educated there and in France. During his student days in Paris he was prompted to write his first two novels, *Une Vie de Boy* and *Le Vieux Nègre et la Médaille*, both published in 1956, and he was also active and successful on the stage and on television. On his return to Yaoundé and after the independence of Cameroon in 1960, he joined the Diplomatic Service. He has since represented his country at the European Common Market and has been ambassador to Liberia, France and the United States as well as Director General of UNICEF at the United Nations headquarters in New York. Since the publication of his first two novels, Ferdinand Oyono published *Chemin d'Europe* in 1960, and all his work has been widely translated from French.

Houseboy

FERDINAND OYONO

Houseboy

Translated from the French by

JOHN REED

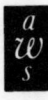

HEINEMANN

Heinemann Educational Publishers
Halley Court, Jordan Hill, Oxford OX2 8EJ
Part of Harcourt Education Limited

Heinemann is the registered trademark of
Harcourt Education Limited

Heinemann Publishers (Pty) Limited
PO Box 781940, Sandton 2146, Johannesburg, South Africa

First published in France as
Une Vie de Boy 1960
© Editions Julliard 1960

This translation first published 1966
© John Reed 1966
First published in *African Writers Series* 1966
First published in this edition 1990

10-digit ISBN: 0 435905 32 5
13-digit ISBN: 978 0 435905 32 3

*This edition has been completely reset and page numbers do
not now correspond with earlier editions*

Printed and bound in Great Britain by
Cox & Wyman Ltd, Reading, Berkshire

06   19

It was evening. The sun had gone down from behind the high peaks. The deep shadow of the forest was closing in around Akomo. Flocks of toucans cut the air with great wingbeats and their plaintive calls died slowly away. The last night of my holiday in Spanish Guinea came stealthily down. Soon I would be leaving this country used by us 'Frenchmen' from Gabon and the Cameroons as a place to slip away for a break whenever things became a little strained between ourselves and our white compatriots.

It was the time of day for the customary meal of fish and cassava sticks. We eat in silence, for while the mouth speaks it does not serve for eating. The eyes of the housedog sprawled between my legs followed, full of envy, piece after piece of fish down the throat of his master, my host. We all ate our fill. At the end of the meal with our little fingers we scratched our bellies each in turn.* The mistress of the house thanked us with a smile. The evening would be full of merriment and forest stories. We pretended to forget that I was soon going away. I gave myself up to the spontaneous gaiety of my hosts whose only thought now was to gather round the fireside and tell over the endless adventures of the tortoise and the elephant.

'There is no moon,' said my host, 'or we would have danced in honour of your departure.'

'We could make a bonfire in the courtyard,' suggested his wife.

'I did not think of it during the day, there is no more wood.'

His wife sighed. Suddenly there was a sinister roll of drums. I could not understand the drum language used by my Spanish

* A polite indication that one has eaten well.

friends but I knew from the troubled looks on their faces that the drums spoke of some misfortune.

'*Madre de Dios,*' said Anton, crossing himself.

His wife turned up her eyes until the pupils vanished. She too crossed herself. Without thinking I brought my hand up to my forehead.

'*Madre Dios,*' said Anton again. He turned towards me. 'Another poor Frenchman ... it says a Frenchman is very ill. They do not think he will last the night.'

This man was nothing to me. I did not even know him. Yet my mind was deeply disturbed. It is strange. A message of death like this in the Cameroons would have woken no more than a shadow of emotion in me – the distant pity we feel when the hour of death has come for someone else. Here, on Spanish soil, I was overwhelmed.

'The drum comes from M'foula, which is very strange,' said my host. 'There are no Frenchmen at M'foula that I know of. The dying man must have come this morning. We shall know tomorrow.'

I felt them all watching me with that look of silent compassion which our people can give their eyes. I stood up and asked Anton if M'foula was very far.

'Just the other side of the great forest ... the lamp is full of paraffin.'

He saw into my heart and read what was written there.

We set out armed with spears. A boy went in front with an old hurricane lamp that threw a pale and feeble light on our path. We passed through two villages. The people we met who recognized Anton asked what it was that called us out to travel at night. They spoke a jargon of Spanish mixed with Pahouin. Several times I caught the word 'frances'. Everyone crossed himself. Then as they left us, they suddenly forgot these dramatics and shouted a jovial 'Buenas tardes' after us. Our path went deeper into the forest.

'Tired already?' said Anton to me. 'The journey is just starting.'

2

At last our path left the forest and wound its way across a heath among tall essessongo trees. The sound of the drum grew more and more distinct. We came out into a clearing. The gloomy hoot of an owl broke one of the intermittent silences that followed the muffled beating of the drum. Anton gave a great shout of laughter that echoed and re-echoed among the giant forest trees. He began to hurl insults after the bird as if he were abusing another human being.

'It's poor Pedro,' he said, between gusts of laughter. 'The dog. He died a fortnight ago. When we fetched a priest to save his soul, he told him to fuck off. His wife even burnt his finger-nails to try and bring him round to a conversion. But nothing doing. The old bugger stuck it out. He died a heathen. Now he's turned into an owl and he's dying of cold in the depths of this forest. Only the priest can do anything now, if his widow decides to have a Mass said after all. . . . Poor old Pedro!'

I made no reply to this lesson in metempsychosis delivered in the night, deep in an equatorial forest. We skirted a bush fire and arrived. M'foula was like all the other villages we had passed; huts thatched with raffia, with whitewashed walls, arranged around a courtyard foul with the droppings of animals. The dark mass of the *aba** stood out against the night. There was a great bustle and disturbance. We went inside.

The dying man lay on a bamboo bed. His eyes were haggard. He was curled up, folded into himself like a huge antelope. His shirt was covered with blood.

'This stench will make us ill,' someone said.

I had never seen a man die. There was a man before me, in pain, and I saw him utterly untransfigured by any glimmer of the after-life. He looked as if he might still summon the stubborn energy not to go on the great journey.

He coughed. Blood ran out from between his lips. The boy who had come with us put down his lamp beside the dying man. With a superhuman effort he struggled to cover his eyes. I moved the lamp away from him and turned down the wick.

* The hut used for discussions.

3

The man was young. I bent over and asked him if there was anything he wanted. There was a nauseating stench of decay. I lit a cigarette. The man turned towards me. As he took me in detail by detail he seemed to come out of the coma he had been in when we arrived. He smiled faintly and then coughed again. He stretched out a trembling hand and stroked the knee of my trousers.

'A Frenchman, a Frenchman,' he panted. 'You are from the Cameroons ...?'

I nodded.

'I knew it, I recognized you were, brother, by your face. ... Some arki, I want some arki.'

A woman passed me a cup full of a kind of rum smelling of smoke. I poured it into his mouth. He was a connoisseur. In spite of his pain he gave me a wink. He seemed to have gathered strength again. Even before he had called out to me to help him sit up he had begun to lift himself on his elbow. I put my arm round his shoulders and drew him up so that he could lean his back against the wall. His vacant eyes suddenly shone. They never left me.

'Brother,' he said. 'Brother, what are we? What are we blackmen who are called French?'

His voice grew bitter. I had never asked myself the question. I was young then and thoughtless. I felt myself grow stupid.

'You see, brother,' he went on, 'I'm finished ... they've got me ...' He showed me his shoulder. 'Still I'm glad I'm dying well away from where they are. My mother always used to say what my greediness would bring me to in the end ... If I had known it would bring me to my grave ... She was right, my poor mother.'

A hiccup shook him and his head dropped on to his shoulder. He cleared his throat.

'I am from the Cameroons, my friend, I am a Maka ... I'd have made old bones if I'd been good and stayed at home in the village.'

His mind began to wander. He was interrupted by a fit of

coughing, then once more his breathing grew normal. I helped him to lie down again. He drew his wasted arms on to his breast and crossed them. We were soon forgotten as he contemplated the mats of the roof, blackened by soot. I turned up the wick of the lamp where the flame had begun to flicker. It lit up the side of the bamboo bed on which the dying man lay. His shadow was thrown on to the cracked wall of the *aba*. Two spiders were running over it. Their enormously exaggerated shadows looked like two octopuses whose tentacles hung down like the branches of a willow tree weeping over the ape-like shadow of the dying man's head. Spasms seized him. He shuddered and expired. He could not be kept till morning and they buried him directly, that night. He was already rotten before he died.

I learnt that they had found him unconscious close to the frontier in the Spanish zone. A khaki bundle was handed over to me.

The man who had found it said gravely, 'He must have been *uno alumno*.'

I opened the packet. Inside there were two worn exercise books, a toothbrush, a stub of pencil and a large native comb made of ivory.

That was how I came to read Toundi's diary. It was written in Ewondo which is one of the main languages of the Cameroons. In the translation which I have made and which you are about to read, I have tried to keep the richness of the original language without letting it get in the way of the story itself.

First
Exercise Book

AUGUST

Father Gilbert says I can read and write fluently. Now I can keep a diary like he does. Keeping a diary is a white man's custom and what pleasure there is in it I do not know. But I shall try it out.

While my master and benefactor was hearing confessions, I had a look into his diary. Ah, it is a grain-store for memories. These white men can preserve everything. In Father Gilbert's diary I found the kick he gave me when he caught me mimicking him in the sacristy. I felt my bottom burning all over again. It is strange, I thought I had forgotten all about it. . . .

* * *

My name is Toundi Ondoua. I am the son of Toundi and of Zama. When the Father baptized me he gave me the name of Joseph. I am Maka by my mother and Ndjem by my father. My ancestors were cannibals. Since the white men came we have learnt other men must not be looked upon as animals.

They say in the village that I was the cause of my father's death because I ran away to a white priest on the day before initiation when I should have met the famous serpent who watches over all the men of my race. Father Gilbert believes it was the Holy Spirit that led me to him. In fact I just wanted to get close to the white man with hair like the beard on a maize cob who dressed in woman's clothes and gave little black boys sugar lumps. I was in a gang of heathen boys who followed the missionary about as he went from hut to hut trying to make converts to the new religion. He knew a few words of Ndjem but his pronunciation was so bad that the way he said them, they all had obscene meanings. This amused everybody and his success was assured. He threw the little lumps of sugar to us like throwing corn to chickens. What a battle to get hold of one of those little white lumps! They were worth all the scraped knees, swollen eyes and painful cuts. Sometimes these distributions of sugar turned into brawls between our parents. One day my mother got into a fight with the mother of my friend Tinati because he had twisted my arm to make me let go of two lumps of sugar which I had won at the cost of a bleeding nose. That battle nearly came to bloodshed. My father had to be restrained by the neighbours from splitting open the head of Tinati's father, while Tinati's father was threatening to put his assegai through my father's stomach. When they had both been calmed down, my father, armed with a cane, invited me to follow him behind the house.

'You, Toundi, are the cause of this whole business. Your greediness will be the ruin of us. Anyone would think you don't have enough to eat at home. So on the day before your initiation you have to cross a stream to go begging lumps of sugar from some white man-woman who is a complete stranger to you.'

My father however was not a stranger and I was well acquainted with what he could do with a stick. Whenever he went for either my mother or me, it always took us a week to recover. I was a good way from his stick. He swished it in the air and came towards me. I edged backwards.

'Are you going to stop? I've not got legs to go chasing you. You know if I don't get you now I will wait for you for a hundred years to give you your punishment. Now come here and get it over with.'

'I haven't done anything to be beaten for, father,' I protested.

'Aaaaaaaaaaakiaaaaay!' he roared. 'You dare to say you haven't done anything? If you weren't such a glutton, if you hadn't the blood of the gluttons that flows through your mother's veins you wouldn't have been in Fia to fight like the little rat you are over the bits of sugar that cursed white man gives you. You wouldn't have got your arm twisted, your mother wouldn't have had a fight and I wouldn't have wanted to split open Tinati's old father's head. . . . I warn you, you had better stop. If you go one more step backwards, that will be an insult to me. I will take it as a sign that you are capable of taking your mother to bed.'

I stopped. He flung himself on me and the cane swished down on to my bare shoulders. I twisted like a worm in the sun.

'Turn round and put up your arms. I don't want to knock your eye out.'

'Let me off, father,' I begged, 'I won't do it again.'

'You always say that when I start to give you a thrashing. But today I'm going to go on thrashing and thrashing until I'm not angry any more.'

I couldn't cry out because that might have attracted the neighbours. My friends would have thought me a girl. I would have lost my place in the group of 'boys-who-are-soon-to-be-men'. My father gave me another blow that I dodged neatly.

'If you dodge again it means you are capable of taking my mother, your grandmother, to bed.'

My father always used this blackmail to stop me from getting away and to make me submit to his blows.

'I have not insulted you and I am not capable of taking my mother to bed or yours and I won't be beaten any more, so there.'

'How dare you speak to me like that! A drop of my own liquid speaking to me like that! Unless you stand still at once, I shall curse you.'

My father was choking. I had never seen him so furious. I went on backing away from him. He came on after me, down behind the huts, for a good hundred yards.

'Very well then,' he said. 'We'll see where you spend the night. I will tell your mother you have insulted us both. Your way back into the house will pass through my anus.'

With that he turned his back. I did not know where I could go. I had an uncle I did not like because of his scabies. His wife smelt of bad fish and so did he. I hated going into their house. It was growing dark. You could begin to see the flashing light of the fireflies. The thud of mortars announced the preparation of the evening meal. I went back softly behind our house and peered through the cracks in the mud wall. My father had his back to me. My unpleasant uncle was facing him. They were eating. ... The aroma of porcupine made my mouth water. It had been caught in one of my father's traps and we had found it half eaten by ants two days later. My mother was famous in the village for her cooking of porcupine.

'The very first of the season,' said my uncle with his mouth full.

My father did not speak but pointed with his finger above his head to where the skulls of the animals he had taken in his traps were hung up in a row.

'You can eat it all up,' said my mother, 'I've kept some for Toundi in the pot.'

My father leapt up, stammering with rage. I saw there would be a storm.

'Bring Toundi's share here,' he shouted. 'He's not to have any of this porcupine. I will teach him to disobey me.'

'But he hasn't had anything since this morning. What will he eat when he gets in?'

'Nothing at all,' said my father.

'If you want to make him obedient,' added my uncle, 'take away his food ... this porcupine is really delicious.'

My mother got up and fetched the pot. I saw my father's hand and my uncle's hand go in. Then I heard my mother crying. For the first time in my life I thought of killing my father.

I went back to Fia ... and after hesitating for a long while I knocked at the white priest's door. I found him in the middle of his dinner. He was very surprised. I tried to explain through signs that I wanted to go away with him. He laughed with all his teeth so his mouth looked like a crescent moon. I stood shyly by the door. He made signs that I should come closer and he offered me what was left of his meal. I found it strange and delicious. We continued a conversation by signs. I knew I had been accepted.

That is how I became Father Gilbert's boy.

My father heard the news next day. I was afraid of how angry he would be ... I explained to the priest, still using signs. He was amused. He gave me a friendly pat on the shoulder. I felt protected.

In the afternoon my father came. All he said to me was that I was still his son, the drop of his liquid and that he bore me no grudge. If I came home, everything would be forgotten. I knew just how much trust I could put in a speech like this made in front of the white man. I put my tongue out at him. The look came into his eye that always came when he was going to 'teach me how to behave'. But I was not afraid while Father Gilbert was there. Father Gilbert's eyes seemed to cast a spell over my father. He lowered his head and went out crestfallen.

My mother came to see me that night. She was crying. We cried together. She told me I had done well to leave my father's house and that my father did not love me as a father ought to love his son. She said that she gave me her blessing and that if ever I fell ill I had only to bathe in a stream and I would be cured.

Father Gilbert gave me a pair of khaki shorts and a red jersey. All the boys in Fia were so impressed by these that they came to ask Father Gilbert to take them on as well.

Two days later Father Gilbert took me on his motor-cycle. We spread panic through the villages by the noise we made. His tour had lasted a fortnight and now we were on our way back to the Saint Peter's Catholic Mission at Dangan. I was happy. The speed intoxicated me. I was going to learn about the city and white men and live like them. I caught myself thinking I was like one of the wild parrots we used to attract to the village with grains of maize. They were captured through their greediness. My mother often used to say, laughing, 'Toundi, what will your greediness bring you to . . .?'

My parents are dead. I have never been back to the village.

*   *   *

Now I am at the Saint Peter's Catholic Mission at Dangan. I wake up every morning at five o'clock and even earlier sometimes when all the priests are at the Mission. I ring the little bell hung at the entrance to the sacristy, then I wait for the first father to come for Mass. I serve up to three or four Masses every day. The skin on my knees is now as hard as crocodile skin. When I kneel down I seem to be kneeling on cushions.

I like the distribution of Communion on Sundays best of all. All the faithful come up to the altar rail with their eyes shut, and their mouths open and their tongues stuck out as if they were pulling a face. The Europeans receive Communion separately. They haven't got nice teeth. I like stroking the white girls under the chin with the paten I am holding for them while the priest pops the host into the mouths. The houseboy of a priest from Yaoundé taught me that trick. It's the only chance we'll ever get of stroking them. . . .

An old woman from the Sixa* gets our food. We prefer the leavings from the priests' meals. Sometimes we find scraps of meat there.

*   *   *

Everything I am I owe to Father Gilbert. He is my benefactor and I am very fond of him. He is cheerful and pleasant and when I was small he treated me like a pet animal. He loved to pull my ears and all the time I have been getting an education he has loved to watch my constant amazement at everything.

He presents me to the whites who visit the Mission as his

* A kind of boarding house for women who are intending to become Christians and for Christian women who have left their pagan families.

14

masterpiece. I am his boy, a boy who can read and write, serve Mass, lay a table, sweep out his room and make his bed. I don't earn any money. Now and then he gives me an old shirt or an old pair of trousers. Father Gilbert knew me when I was stark naked, he taught me to read and write. . . . Nothing can be more precious than that, even if I have to go badly dressed.

* * *

Today Father Vandermayer came back from the bush. He has brought five women with him. It seems they are Christians that he has taken away from their polygamous husband. Five more boarders for the Sixa. If they knew the work there is waiting for them here, they would have stayed behind with their husband.

Father Vandermayer is Father Gilbert's assistant. He has the best voice in the Mission so he sings Mass at the major feasts. But he is rather a funny person, Father Vandermayer. On a Sunday when he isn't singing the High Mass he won't let anyone else take the collection. One day when I had taken it he made me come to his room. Then he undressed me and searched me. He made one of the catechists stay with me all through the day in case I had swallowed any of the coins.

He is censor for the houseboys and the faithful of the parish. He has never managed to catch me out. I could never stand what he does to people who have misbehaved. He loves to beat the Christians who have committed adultery — native Christians of course. . . . He makes them undress in his office while he repeats in bad Ndjem, 'When you were kissing, weren't you ashamed before God?' Sunday after Mass has become a terrible time for everyone who has Father Vandermayer as spiritual director.

* * *

I saw a very pretty girl at the blacks' communion. I stroked her under the chin with the paten like we do the white girls. She opened one eye, then shut it again. She really must come to Communion again.

* * *

Father Vandermayer has been down with a bout of malaria. He shouted obscenities all night. Father Gilbert has told us not to hang about near his room.

* * *

My father, my benefactor, Father Gilbert is dead. They found him bloody and crushed on his motor cycle by the side of a branch from the giant cotton tree that the natives call the 'Hammer of the whites'. They say two white men, Greeks, had already suffered the same fate as Father Gilbert. On a windless day the cotton tree dropped one of its branches like a gigantic club on the Greeks' car just at the moment it was passing underneath. All they found afterwards were two pulpy masses in drill suits amongst the twisted metal. The Commandant who was at Dangan at that time talked about having the cotton tree cut down. But after the Greeks were buried the whole thing was forgotten . . . until this morning.

Every Thursday Father Gilbert used to go into Dangan so that he could collect the mail for the Mission personally. How pleased he used to be at the thought of a letter from home. As soon as we had finished the main service he would rush to the garage to get out the motor cycle. Then he would call to me to hold it while he tucked his cassock up to his waist, showing his hairy legs and khaki shorts. When he was ready he would take the machine and drop heavily into the saddle. I would push it till the noise of the engine became steady. Then he would disappear at high speed leaving behind a cloud of fumes and dust and a smell of petrol that turned my stomach over.

This morning, the motor cycle was more difficult than ever to get started. Father Gilbert got off several times and fiddled with something in the engine. I was bathed in sweat from pushing him. He was cursing and swearing and calling the motor cycle names. I had never seen him so on edge. At last after one or two sudden starts and then a thunderous noise, he burst away and I caught a glimpse of him through the dust, his body bent slightly forward disappearing at a speed like a thing bewitched. . . . Who could have told me then that was to be my last image of Father Gilbert?

It was about ten o'clock when the head catechist, the one Father Vandermayer had set to watch me, came howling up to the gate of the priests' villa. He rolled about on the ground shouting 'Father . . . Father . . .' Out rushed Father Vandermayer with such a stream of abuse as only he could produce. I thought Martin must be drunk. They said he rolled about like that in his hut when he had been drinking. Father Vandermayer opened the gate swearing and grabbed Martin by the coat.

'Father . . . Father . . . is . . . is . . . dead,' stammered Martin, '. . . in . . . in . . .'

Father Vandermayer stopped him short. He gave him a kick and pointed to the path leading to the Mission workers' compound.

'Go and get drunk somewhere else! Go and get drunk at home!' roared Father Vandermayer giving him a push in the back.

At that moment the hospital ambulance appeared in the courtyard of the church, followed closely by all the cars in Dangan. My blood drained away, my knees buckled. . . .

No, it could not be true that Father Gilbert was dead. . . .

I ran towards the ambulance, towards the stretcher. The white man who had been everything in the world to me lay there. I collided with a white man with a long neck, then with another, a hulking yellowish man. They pushed me back, one with the whip he always carried, the other feinted a kick. . . .

The whole of Saint Peter's Mission was there. The Sixa women had pushed their way through the old catechists and surrounded the group of whites, weeping. Everybody who wanted to show how attached he had been to the dead Father was there. Workers forcing out their tears. You could see their contorted faces the difficulty they were having to make their eyes wet. Stupid-looking catechists uncertainly stroking their rosaries, starry-eyed catechumens hoping that perhaps they would be lucky enough to be present at a miracle. Labourers who looked so miserable that Father Vandermayer would hardly have the heart to stop them the day's pay. But most of the crowd was there because they had never had a chance before to see a white man's corpse – still less the corpse of a white priest. All these people kept up a squealing round the group of white men. The long-necked white man spoke to one of the constables who was in his car. The constable counted out ten paces walking against the crowd and the crowd fell back at each step, once, twice, three times . . . up to ten. Two orderlies carried Father Gilbert's body into his room. The Europeans followed it in. Father Vandermayer led them into the sitting-room. A few moments later he came out again, down the steps. He spoke to the crowd.

'The Father of us all,' he began, rubbing his fingers together, 'the Father of us all is dead. Pray for him, my brothers, pray for him, for God is just, he gives to every man his due. . . .'

He stroked his hair, then went on to give his orders.

'Go to the church . . . Pray for him, my brothers. Pray for him, the Father of all of us who will rest in this Mission, among you all that he loved so much . . .'

He rubbed his eyes. The howls redoubled.

'God is just,' he went on. 'He is everlasting. His will be done.'

He made the sign of the cross and the crowd copied him. He went up the steps. At the top step his hands came down to his thighs and straightened his cassock.

Martin, the head catechist, was crying at my side. I do not

know why he was there instead of leading the other catechists in their prayers. He had unbuttoned his old coat and his tears ran down his wrinkled belly underneath the knot he had tied in his loin-cloth over his grizzled pubic hairs.

'There is nothing left for me but to go away,' he intoned. 'There is nothing left except to die. . . . I knew someone was going to die, the chimpanzees howled all night. There is nothing left for me but to go away. Nothing except to die. . . .'

The crowd was swallowed up in the church. The Europeans went away. One stayed behind to supervise the carpenters who came across the courtyard with planks and sheet-iron. Two constables with fixed bayonets marched up and down the veranda outside the room where the body lay.

The funeral will be at four tomorrow. Twice the constables have made me move off. Father Vandermayer has not said anything. . . .

AFTER THE FUNERAL

My benefactor was buried in the corner of the cemetery reserved for Europeans. The grave of Father Gilbert lies next to the grave of M. Diamond's daughter – the one he had by his mistress and acknowledged. Father Vandermayer said the burial service. All the Europeans in Dangan were there, even the Americans from the Protestant Mission.

It is only now that I realize that Father Gilbert is dead. I have not heard his voice since yesterday. The Catholic Mission is in mourning. But for me, it is more than mourning. I have died my first death. . . .

I saw the girl from communion at the funeral. She shut her eyes again. She is stupid.

* * *

The new Commandant needs a boy. Father Vandermayer told me to report to the Residence tomorrow. I am glad because I have not been able to bear life at the Mission since Father Gilbert died. Of course it is a good riddance for Father Vandermayer as well.

I shall be the Chief European's boy. The dog of the King is the King of dogs.

I shall leave the Mission this evening. From now on I shall live with my brother-in-law in the location. A new life is starting for me.

O Lord, Thy will be done . . .

* * *

At last it has happened. The Commandant has definitely taken me into his service. It was midnight, I had finished my work and was getting ready to go back to the location when the Commandant told me to follow him into his office. It was a terrible moment for me.

After he had looked at me for a long while, he asked me point-blank if I were a thief.

'No, Sir,' I answered.

'Why aren't you a thief?'

'Because I do not want to go to hell.'

He seemed taken aback by my answer. He tossed his head in disbelief.

'Where did you learn that?'

'I am a Christian, Sir,' I told him, and proudly showed him the St Christopher medal I wear round my neck.

'So, you are not a thief because you don't want to go to hell?'

'Yes, Sir.'

'What is it like, hell?'

'Well, Sir, it is flames and snakes and the Devil with horns. There is a picture of hell in my prayer book ... I ... I ... can show it to you.'

I was going to pull the little prayer book out of the back pocket of my shorts but the Commandant made a sign to stop me. He watched me for a minute through the wreathes of smoke he was puffing into my face. He sat down. I bowed my head. I could feel his eyes on me. He crossed his legs and uncrossed them. He signalled me to a chair opposite to him. He leant towards me and lifted up my chin. He gazed into my eyes and went on.

'Good, good, Joseph, we shall be friends.'

'Yes, Sir. Thank you, Sir.'

'But if you steal, I shan't wait till you go to hell. It's too far ...'

'Yes, sir. It's ... Where is it, sir?'

I had never asked myself the question. My master was amused to see my puzzlement. He shrugged and leant against the back of his chair.

'So you don't know where this hell is where you're afraid you'll go and burn?'

'It's next to Purgatory, Sir. It's . . . It's . . . in the sky.'

My master smothered a laugh. Then, serious again, he pierced me with his panther eyes.

'Well done! There we are then. I think you see why I can't wait till "small Joseph go burn in hell".'

The Commandant imitated the pidgin used by native soldiers. He put on a strange voice. I thought he was very funny. I coughed hard so as not to laugh. He went on, not noticing.

'If you steal from me I shall skin you alive.'

'Yes, Sir. I know, Sir. I didn't say that just now, Sir, because I took that for granted, Sir . . .'

'All right, all right,' said the Commandant, impatiently.

He got up and began to walk round me.

'You're a clean lad,' he said, looking me over carefully. 'No jiggers. Your shirt is clean, No scabies.'

He stepped back and looked me up and down again.

'You're intelligent. The priests speak very well of you. So I can count on little Joseph, eh?'

'Yes, Sir,' I said. My eyes shone with pleasure and pride.

'You may go. Be here every morning at six o'clock. You understand?'

When I was outside on the veranda I felt I had just come through a hard battle. The end of my nose was perspiring.

My master is thickset. His legs have great muscles like the legs of a pedlar. He is the kind of man we call 'mahogany-trunk' because the trunk of the mahogany tree is so strong that it never bends in a storm. I am not a storm. I am the thing that obeys.

*   *   *

At midday I watched my master from the kitchen window. He was climbing the huge flight of steps up to the front of the

Residence. It didn't seem to tire him as it does the cook and me. His strength seemed to increase as he went up.

From the sitting-room his sharp voice came demanding a beer. As I ran to serve him my cap rolled across the floor to his feet. In a flash I saw his eyes grow as small as a cat's eyes in the sun. He stamped his foot and the floorboards resounded like a drum. I was turning to go to the refrigerator when he pointed to the cap at his foot. I was nearly dead with fear.

'Are you going to pick it up?'

'In a moment, Sir.'

'What are you waiting for?'

'I will bring you your beer first, Sir.'

'But . . .' Then he said gently, 'Take your time.'

I took a step towards him then I came back towards the refrigerator. I could feel the Commandant near me, the smell of him getting stronger and stronger.

'Pick up your cap.'

Feebly I bent to pick it up. The Commandant grabbed me by the hair, swung me round and peered into my eyes.

'I'm not a monster . . . but I wouldn't like to disappoint you.'

With that he shot out a kick to my shins that sent me sprawling under the table. The Commandant's kick was even more painful than the kick of the late father Gilbert. He seemed pleased with his effort. He moved about restlessly. Then he asked me in a flat voice if I was now ready to get his beer. I gave a weak smile but he was no longer noticing. When I had brought him his beer he got up and put his hand on my shoulder.

'Joseph,' he said, 'be a man and, above all, think what you are doing. Right?'

I took off my apron at midnight. I wished the Commandant good night.

*　　*　　*

Last night the location had a visit from Gullet, the Chief of Police. He gets his name from his long flexible neck like a tickbird's neck. Anyway, Gullet and his men came down to the African location. I had left the Residence at midnight. When I got home, everyone was asleep. I lay down but couldn't get to sleep. I shut my eyes and waited for sleep to come. A time came when I didn't know if I were asleep or awake. In a dream I heard the screeching of brakes. The house was flooded with light as if it were full moon. I got up and went softly to the door. Someone outside was hammering on it violently.

'Open up, open up,' I heard.

I stole back to go and warn my brother-in-law. I was surprised to find he was already awake.

'It's Gullet and his men,' I whispered in his ear.

We went to open the door where our visitors were giving such indications of their impatience. The door gave way before I could open it. Into the tiny house charged four Ful'be constables followed by Gullet. I slipped behind the door while my brother-in-law and sister, half dead with fear, watched Gullet and his men overturning the bits of furniture. They upset the old petrol tin and the water that was in it went over my sleeping mat. Gullet kicked a water jug that shattered into pieces. He told one of his men to turn over a pile of banana bunches. He pulled off a banana and gobbled it down. I trembled for my sister, her eyes fixed on the white man's enormous Adam's apple. It swelled and subsided like a bellows as Gullet swallowed the banana down. He threw the skin away and swung round twice on his heels. Then he pointed at us. The constable with the red braid dragged me from behind the door and pushed me in front of his chief. Gullet shone his powerful electric torch into my face. I blinked and instinctively pushed my head back.

'Name,' said the African N.C.O. who was acting as interpreter.

'Toundi.'

'Toundi what?' said the police chief.

'Toundi Joseph, the Commandant's boy.'

Gullet frowned. The N.C.O. confirmed what I had said with a 'It is truth, sah.'

The white man turned his back on me and directed the beam of light into the shadows where my brother-in-law and sister were hiding.

'It is my sister and the man who is her husband.'

'It is truth, sah,' said the N.C.O. again.

'Good,' said Gullet with an angry glance at the African policeman. 'Good, good,' he said, looking at us each in turn.

He picked another banana and began to eat it. My sister's eyes grew round. I began to be afraid again. Gullet turned, bent his long neck and went out. The noise of the engines died away and then there was silence.

All the Africans had gone into the forest. It was the African N.C.O. who had warned the whole location by blowing his whistle when they arrived at our house. Gullet did not catch anyone in last night's raid. He ate some bananas.

* * *

I woke up at first cockcrow. Everyone was still asleep when I reached the Residence except the sentry. I could hear him walking up and down on the veranda. He recognized me and came over. We sat down on the entrance steps and he asked me what I thought of Panther-Eye. 'Ah,' I thought, 'so that's what they call the Commandant.'

'Man,' said the sentry, 'Panther-Eye beat like Gullet. Him kick me bam! Go like dynamite. Panther-Eye no joke.'

'Yes,' I said, 'Panther-Eye has got us ...'

The police-camp bugle sounded six o'clock. I heard a tremendous roar of 'Boy, my shower.' For a European, my master is a very early riser. Later, when he came back from the shower, he asked me if I had slept well.

'Yes, Sir,' I said.

'Really?' said the Commandant, a smile at the corner of his mouth.

'Yes, Sir,' I said again.

'Liar,' he said.

'I am not, Sir.'

'Liar,' he said.

'I am not, Sir.'

'What about the raid last night?'

He shrugged. Then he said I was a poor sod. He swallowed his coffee painfully and swore at the cook. There wasn't enough sugar in it. He gave us our daily designation of 'You idle shower of loafers' and left the house, slamming the door behind him.

Today is Saturday. The whites in Dangan usually spend their Saturdays at the European Club which is run by M. Janopoulos. All the houseboys are free at twelve.

On my way back to the location I met Sophie, the African mistress of the agricultural engineer. She seemed angry about something.

'What's wrong with a day off?' I asked her.

'I am a proper fool,' she said. 'The one day my white man leaves the keys of his strongbox in his trouser pocket during siesta is the day I don't go through them.'

'You want to stop him going back to his own country?'

'Fuck his country and fuck him. It makes me sick when I think of all the time I've been going with the uncircumcized sod and what have I made out of it? Now today comes my real chance and I miss it ... I must have mud between my ears instead of brains ...'

'Ah, don't you love your white man? He's the most handsome white man in Dangan you know.'

She looked at me for a moment and retorted.

'You talk as if you weren't black. You know very well, whites haven't got what we can fall in love with ...'

'So?'

'So what? I'm waiting ... waiting my chance; and then Sophie is off to Spanish Guinea ... Well, what do you expect? We don't mean anything to them either. It's a good job it's mutual. Only I'm sick and tired of hearing "Sophie, don't come today. I've got a European coming to see me at the house," "Sophie, you can come, the European has gone," "Sophie, when you see me with a white lady don't look at me, don't greet me," and all the rest.'

We walked on side by side without speaking, thinking our own thoughts.

'What a fool I am,' she said again as she went off.

About five o'clock in the evening I went to hang about outside the European Club. There were a fair number of Africans there to watch the whites enjoying themselves. M. Janopoulos organizes all the entertainments for the European population of Dangan. He has been here longer than any of them though the exact date he came here is the subject of great speculation. There is a story that he is the sole survivor from a party of adventurers who were eaten in the eastern region of the country a few years before the First World War. Since then, M. Janopoulos who might well have finished up inside someone's stomach has got on in the world. . . . He is now the wealthiest member of the European community in Dangan. M. Janopoulos doesn't like natives. He likes to set his huge Alsatian on them. This causes a great stampede and amuses the ladies.

Such amusement was provided today. The crowd of Africans who had come to watch the whites was denser than usual. Massed near the European Club we were beginning to infiltrate into the clump of essessongo trees, when M. Janopoulos indulged in his favourite sport. The usual stampede soon became a frenzied rout. The numbers of the sightseers had been doubled by the knowledge that the new Commandant was to be at the Club. At the first alarm I was jostled, then knocked down and trampled on. I could feel the Greek's dog at my heels. I shall never know how I managed to get to my feet and to climb up to the top of the huge mango tree. There I took refuge. The

Europeans were laughing and pointing up to the top of the tree where I was hiding. The Commandant was laughing as well. He had not recognized me. How could he recognize me? All Africans look the same to them.

When I arrived at the Residence this morning I was surprised to see the cook had got there before me. I heard a familiar fit of coughing. The Commandant was having his shower. He called to me through the bathroom door which was ajar. He sent me to fetch a bottle from beside his bed. I came back a few seconds later and knocked on the bathroom door. The Commandant told me to come in. He was naked under the shower.

I felt a strange embarrassment.

'Well, did you get the bottle?' he shouted. . . . 'Well . . . what is the matter with you?' he said.

'Nothing . . . nothing, sir,' I said. My throat felt tight.

He came towards me and snatched the bottle out of my hands. I backed out of the bathroom. The Commandant made a vague gesture and shrugged his shoulders.

No, it can't be true, I told myself, I couldn't have seen properly. A great chief like the Commandant uncircumcized.

He had seemed to me more naked than my fellow Africans who strip unconcerned and wash at the water channel in the market place. So, I told myself, he is like Father Gilbert! Like Father Vandermayer! Like Sophie's lover!

I was relieved by this discovery. It killed something inside me. . . . I knew I should never be frightened of the Commandant again. When he called to me to bring his sandals his voice sounded far-off. I seemed to be hearing it for the first time. I wondered why I used to tremble in his presence.

My coolness surprised him. I took my time over whatever he told me to do. He shouted at me as he always did but I did not move. His eyes had once struck panic into me. Now I stood unconcerned under their gaze.

'Have you turned into a complete nincompoop?' he snapped at me.

I must look that word up in the dictionary.

*   *   *

A prisoner brought two chickens and a basket of eggs up to the Residence. That means the prison-director is back from his tour. All the Europeans in Dangan send something to the Commandant when they come back from the bush. The doctor is the most generous.

I presented the chickens and the eggs to my master. He swallowed two of the eggs raw. I felt sick to watch him. I asked him if he wanted raw eggs at lunchtime. He pointed to the door. . . . I came back though, to help him put on his rubber boots because it was raining. I gave them a final polish. The Commandant trod on my fingers as he went out. I did not cry out. He did not turn round.

*   *   *

I came along this morning with Ondoua, the drummer. It is his job to sound the hours on his drum.

The agricultural engineer made him come from his village to do this work. He gave him a huge alarm clock which he carries about with him everywhere. He carries it tied to a shoulder strap with an old filthy scarf. He always has a gourd full of rum hanging from his left shoulder like a beggar's bag.

I asked him to translate for me the message that he has been playing for two years now to call the labourers. He tossed his head and then, after hesitating for a moment, began.

'What I play goes like this:

> Ken . . . ken . . . ken . . . ken . . .
> Out of bed . . . Out of bed . . .
> Ken . . . ken . . . ken . . . ken . . .
> How he troubles us.
> Ken . . . ken . . . ken . . . ken . . .

He doesn't give a fuck for you
He doesn't give a fuck for anyone . . .
Ken . . . ken . . . ken . . . ken . . .
What can you do to him . . .
There is nothing you can do . . .
Ken . . . ken . . . ken . . . ken . . .
Out of bed . . . Out of bed . . .

Then I sound the hour.'

'What if he asks you to translate what you are playing?'

'It's easy enough to lie to a white man.'

He's a very remarkable person, Ondoua. No particular age. No wife. Only his enormous alarm clock. And his gourd of rum. No one has ever seen him drunk in the street. At nights it seems he changes himself into a gorilla . . . though I can't believe this is true.

* * *

I went along with the Commandant to the Headmaster of the Dangan School, where he had been invited for cocktails. I carried the parcel he was going to give to Mme Salvain. This is a native custom that Europeans have as well, taking something for their hosts.

The Government School is about five minutes from the Residence. We went on foot. I walked behind the Commandant. Europeans always run. The Commandant went as if the teachers were all in deadly danger. The Salvains had set up a table outside in the shade of some tree from their own country which had been planted as part of the ceremony at the time the school was opened.

Mme Salvain wore a dress of red silk which showed off her great behind like the ace of hearts. She had fastened up her hair in a figure of eight and stuck a hibiscus flower in it, as red as her dress. She came forward smiling, stretching out her arms to the Commandant. He took her wrists and kissed them, one after the other. She jumped as if hot coals had been dropped on to her arms. She spoke so quickly that I wondered if it was really French that I could hear.

M. Salvain appeared at a window and came hurrying down the steps. He is a little man, as thin as the lean kine in Pharaoh's dream. He was wearing linen trousers and a shirt open to show his bony chest. His wife introduced the Commandant. I kept back in the distance. My master signalled to me and I gave him the parcel. He presented it to Mme Salvain who seemed embarrassed. She slid a glance towards her husband. She began to protest while her hands were taking the parcel. She gazed warmly at the Commandant who urged her to accept it. She began to thank him.

M. and Mme Salvain drew the Commandant towards the table. Mme Salvain sat down between the two men and M. Salvain called his boy, a very old African, the oldest probably of all the boys in Dangan. He brought the bottles and then withdrew obsequiously. The Salvains began a conversation, competing with each other in speed, wit, gaiety. Mme Salvain seeking for a smile or a compliment leant now towards one now towards the other of the two men.

'What a country,' Mme Salvain was saying, 'rain, heat, no hairdresser ... how one perspires! You must find it a great change from Paris?'

The Commandant raised his eyebrows and emptied his glass.

'You haven't told me about your school,' he said to M. Salvain.

M. Salvain began to flutter and rub his hands. 'I am waiting for you to come and inspect,' he said. 'I am on the point of completing an educational experiment that is quite unprecedented. I shall soon be sending a report of it to Yaoundé. When I came here I found the school full of great louts of twenty and over still trying to get their school certificates. I threw them all out. They were bone idle and most of them had gonorrhoea. The African instructors and pupils were making

31

the girls in the school pregnant. It was like a brothel. Going through the registers I discovered that the youngest pupil to get his school certificate was seventeen. The youngest pupil in the school was nine years old and in the preparatory course. After I had thrown out all these louts who had been failing their certificates I made up an infants' class – there hadn't been such a class here before I came – and I made up this class of children between two years old and six. Young African children are just as intelligent as ours. They said I was mad, that I was a rabble-rouser ... well, in my certificate class there are now twenty pupils of between twelve and fifteen years.'

'That is wonderful,' said my master, 'wonderful. I shall be coming to see you one day very soon ...'

'Things have changed since the last war. But people here don't understand.'

'Except for the children Jacques is educating,' said Mme Salvain, 'all the other natives here are not worth the bother. Idle, thieving, lying ... what patience you need with people like that!'

The Commandant coughed and lit a cigarette. Now I could make out nothing but that glowing red dot in the night which had suddenly fallen.

* * *

The Commandant who for some reason can't go anywhere without a native in the back of his pick-up van, told me to come to Mass with him. As we sped past Africans pulled off their hats anxiously. ... The Commandant's pick-up van is the only one with a little tricolour flag. As we went by we left a trail of ochre dust hanging in the air, sultry at the end of the dry season. When we reached Saint Peter's the church was already surrounded by a tightly packed crowd of natives. It was a seething, many-coloured crowd with white and reds and greens standing out against the black skins. A murmur ran through the crowd at the appearance of the Commandant.

I recognized the sound of the little bell in the sacristy. It was all inseparable from the memory of Father Gilbert who is now called ... the martyr, I suppose because he met his death in Africa.

Father Vandermayer came out to meet the Commandant. He bowed with that peculiar gracefulness of the clergy which laymen can never imitate. The Commandant stretched out his hand. In front of them, the statue of Saint Peter, who had been so blackened by the weather that he could have passed for an African, was perched precariously on a kind of belfry at such an angle that it looked as if before long he would come toppling down.

Other cars arrived. All the Europeans who usually spent their time at the European Club seemed to have arranged to meet at this place of God. There was Gullet with his African sergeant following behind his car. Mme Salvain had concealed her spindly legs inside linen trousers which gave even greater prominence to her huge behind. Again she came towards the Commandant with arms outstretched and again was startled by the performance about kisses on her wrists. The agricultural engineer had brought Ondoua with him, all covered with dust. Next were to be seen the arrivals of the doctor, as proud as ever of his captain's braid, of his wife, of the European who disinfects Dangan with D.D.T., of the Mesdemoiselles Dubois, two enormous young ladies with pigtails and cowboy hats, of the wife of the prison-director together with some Greek ladies come to show off their silk dresses. All these Europeans stood in a circle round the Commandant and Father Vandermayer. The bell was rung again. There is only one door into the nave of the church. This was stormed by the Africans waiting in the court-yard. A few hats came off in the crush. There were cries from women and children. ... The Europeans followed Father Vandermayer through the sacristy.

In the church of Saint Peter at Dangan the whites have their seats in the transept beside the altar. There they can follow the Mass comfortably seated in cane armchairs covered with velvet cushions. Men and women sit shoulder to shoulder. Mme Salvain was sitting next to the Commandant. In the row behind, Gullet and the agricultural engineer leant over as in a single movement towards the two fat girls. Behind them the doctor now and then pushed up the gold braid that hung down from his overlarge epaulettes. His wife, pretending to be lost to the world in the perusal of her missal followed out of the corner of her eye what was going on between Gullet, the agricultural engineer, and the two fat Mesdemoiselles Dubois. From time to time she raised her head to see how far the Commandant and Mme Salvain had got. The doctor when he was not pulling up his gold braid was making impatient sweeps of his hand to catch a fly buzzing around his scarlet ears.

The nave of the church is completely reserved for Africans. They sit on tree trunks instead of benches and these are arranged in two rows. The faithful are supervised by catechists ready to pounce at the least sign of inattention. These servants of God march up and down the central aisle that divides the men from the women, carrying sticks.

At last Father Vandermayer, resplendent in his glittering chasuble and preceded by four African altar boys in red and white, made his entrance. A bell rings. Mass begins. The catechists are busy between the two rows of seats in the nave. The proceedings are directed by means of loud smacks with the palm of the hand against their prayer books. The faithful stand up, kneel, stand up again, sit and stand to the rhythm of these smacking noises. Men and women deliberately turn their backs to be sure they won't look at one another. The catechists watch for the flicker of an eyelid.

Down at the front, Gullet seizes his opportunity at the elevation of the Host to squeeze the hand of his neighbour. Mme Salvain's legs move imperceptibly closer to the Commandant's.

Father Vandermayer at last sings the *Ite missa est*. The Europeans get up and go out through the sacristy. In the nave, the catechists close the door so that the Africans have to stay for the sermon. The African doorkeeper let me out when I announced myself as the Commandant's houseboy. Up in the pulpit Father Vandermayer in his atrocious Ndjem was in his innocence embarking upon a sermon full of obscenities. . . .

*   *   *

The Chiefs of Dangan came to welcome my master. Akoma was the first to arrive.

Akoma is the chief of the Sos. He reigns over ten thousand subjects. He is the only one of the Dangan chiefs who has been to France. He brought back from the journey five gold rings which the Europeans call 'alliances'. He wears them one on each finger of his left hand. He is very proud of his name 'The King of the Rings'. When he is addressed by this name he replies with the following piece:

> 'Akoma King of rings, King of wives,
> White man one ring
> Akoma has more than the white men
> Akoma King of rings, King of wives.'

After that you have to touch his alliances.

He came to the Residence with his train; three wives, a porter to carry his chair and the umbrella, a xylophone player and two bodyguards.

'Son of a dog,' he said to me, 'where is your master?'

He dismissed his train and followed me into the drawing-room. He was wearing a good dark suit but being unable to endure leather shoes in hot weather he had put on plimsols instead. When he entered the drawing-room my master got up and went over to him with his hand outstretched. Akoma grasped it with both hands and swung it from side to side. Every time the Commandant asked him a question he said 'Yes, yes' and clucked like a hen. He was pretending he understood French but in fact he does not understand a word. He was presented in Paris, it seems, as a great friend of France.

Mengueme is an old man as cunning as the tortoise in the fables. He understands and speaks French but always pretends not to. He can drink from sunrise to sunset without the slightest effect.

Mengueme is chief of the Yanyans and is highly respected among his people. He is the only one of the elders who has survived his own generation. He puts on his chief's uniform when he comes to visit the Commandant and takes it off as soon as he is out of the European town. When the Germans made the first war on the French his younger brother was killed fighting the French. When the Germans made the second war on the French his two sons were killed fighting the Germans. 'Life,' he says, 'is like the chameleon, changing colour all the time.'

Mengueme has never been overseas. He is wise without travelling. He belongs to the old days.

* * *

It was a fresh morning. The grass was damp. The drips from the palm trees rattled on to the metal roof of the Residence. Dangan slumbered on beneath the pure coverlet of mist brought down by the early morning rain.

The Commandant, shaved, pomaded and in high spirits was seeing to the loading of the pick-up van. For the first time since he came to Dangan he was wearing a maroon-coloured pullover. The sentry had left his post. His large right foot was pressing down on the pedal of the pump inflating the rear tyres. The driver was standing on the front bumper giving the windscreen a final polish. He went over to the sentry who was grasping his knee laboriously with both hands at each movement of the pump. The driver hammered in the tyres which rang like a taut bowstring.

Then everything was ready the Commandant looked at his watch. He glanced towards the Residence and noticed me.

'Get in,' he said. 'we're going on tour.'

He slammed the door and started up the engine. I had just time to jump up on to the luggage. We drove through the commercial centre of the town. Not a soul to be seen. Gangs of workmen looked surprised and hesitated before they saluted as if they could not remember seeing the Commandant up so early.

The Commandant took the road to the agricultural station. The engineer, wearing black, was waiting for us at the foot of the steps. A thermos flask protruded from the travelling bag in his hand. He got up beside the Commandant. He leant out of the car door towards the villa.

'What are you waiting for? Get in.'

The question was addressed to a shadow that could be heard yawning on the veranda.

'Who is it?' said the Commandant.

'My cook,' said the engineer.

It was Sophie. She seemed ready to fall with sleep as she came down the steps. The engineer shone a torch towards her. Sophie rubbed her eyes and cursed under her breath.

Yet, my God, she was beautiful. Her mahogany skin gleamed like bronze in the light that flooded over it. She adjusted her sandals, then took a few steps forward, uncertain. She went up beside the door of the van where the engineer's arms were hanging out. He pointed to the back. She raised her eyebrows and stuck out her lower lip in a little pout of distaste. But she turned away, put her foot on the rear bumper and gave me her hand.

'Is she in?' called the Commandant.

'All right,' I answered.

Through the door the engineer gave me the travelling bag. The van moved off. Sophie sat down beside me on an empty petrol tin. She was completely enveloped in her cloth. All that could be seen was a thick plait of hair from which hung a piece of black thread. This made a stripe across her smooth forehead like a tattoo mark. She looked straight in front of her as if she did not see the trees that sped dizzily by on either side of the road. The wind was cold. There was a smell of the American tobacco the engineer was smoking in the cabin.

Suddenly we were flung into the air. We came crashing down again on the packing case, our insides in agony.

'Christ. What have they got ... What have other women got that I haven't got? What I want to know is what have other women got that I haven't got?' moaned Sophie.

The road had left the town. The van roared through the neighbouring villages. Africans in coloured cloths showed their surprise when they noticed the little tricolour flag. Sometimes a crowd would come rushing out of a little mud-built chapel with a scrap of railway line hanging on the veranda instead of a bell. Naked little girls came out of a half open door and ran to squat down at the foot of the citronellas that lined the road. A violent swerve nearly flung us over the side.

'Christ,' cried Sophie. 'What have they got that I haven't got?'

She turned towards me. Two big tears were rolling down her cheeks. I laid my arm on hers. She wiped her eyes with her cloth.

'What lovely manners they've got, these whites ... even if it's only among themselves ... my arse is just as delicate as the arses of the ladies they have up in the driver's cabin ...'

Sophie began to cry again. She shut her eyes. Her long wet eyelashes turned into little black tufts of hair. Through the rear window of the cabin the engineer's green eye met mine. He turned his head quickly.

The truck had now left the area that had been soaked by the previous night's rain and was jolting along something between a proper road and a mere track. From time to time we passed a long clearing in the forest. Piles of quarried stones showed work was in progress. In between the cobbles which were meant to be the surface of the road the bush was growing up again. Fruits from the umbrella trees were strewn about. A continuous vibration indicated we were now crossing marshy ground where logs had been laid and covered with laterite to give it consistency. The laterite had turned into an ochre mud-like paint. The truck whinnied, crackled, roared and burst out of these tortuous valleys to go bounding up the sides of precipitous hills. In the back of the truck we were in the power of a kind of swaying dance. Our heads nodded as if we were dropping asleep. A jolt like a hiccup lifted us bodily off the packing case to bring our bottoms smacking down on it a moment later.

Sophie had stopped complaining. She said nothing. Her tears had dried, leaving on her cheeks two streaks of nondescript colour.

It began to grow hot. The truck had just passed a huge ant-hill on which had been scrawled in creosote '60 KMS'. We were going down an interminable hill at high speed. The surface of the road had become quite even. The going was as smooth as on the roads in Dangan itself. Above my head I noticed we were passing under arches of interwoven palm trees. We had reached our destination. The Commandant slowed down. He was leaning out of the window and seemed surprised how neat and clean everything looked. After travelling through the bush for 60 kilometres this was most unexpected. No more holes, no more grass, no more dung. The piles of refuse had disappeared from the gutters. Everything had been cleaned. The cleanness was too complete not to be very recent.

In the distance a drum sounded. Then there came a confused murmur. Obviously some great celebration was being put on for us. At last the village came into view. There was a stir and bustle about it that could hardly be normal. A sea of human beings filled the central square in the village. Shrill cries re-echoed from the women. They ululated with their hands against their mouths. It sounded like the siren on the American sawmill at Dangan. The crowd parted to make way for the truck which came to a standstill in front of a freshly lopped umbrella tree with a French flag fluttering from the top.

An old man with a humped back and a face as deeply wrinkled as the backside of a tortoise opened the door of the truck. The Commandant shook him by the hand. The engineer offered him his hand. The women began to call again. A young man wearing a red chéchia shouted 'Silence!' He was naked to the waist and wore a loin-cloth but the chéchia showed he was the Chief's attendant and gave him his authority. The Chief himself wore a khaki jacket on to the sleeves of which his red badges and their silver braid had been sewn, apparently in some haste. From each sleeve trailed a length of white cotton. A middle-aged man wearing a pyjama top over his loin-cloth shouted 'Eyes front!' Some thirty urchins, unnoticed until now, sprang to attention.

'Forward marsss!' ordered the man.

The schoolboys advanced in front of the Commandant. Their instructor shouted once more. 'Eyes front!' The boys seemed to panic. They huddled together like chickens who have sighted the shadow of a vulture. The instructor gave them the note, then beat out the time. The children sang, without any pauses, in a language which was not their own or French but the strange gibberish which village people suppose is French and Frenchmen suppose is the vernacular. When they had finished everybody clapped.

The Chief led the white men into a hut which had been got ready for them. The ground had been swept, the brush marks were still visible in the kaolin on the walls. The roof was green and freshly thatched with raffia. In the sultry heat the inside of the hut afforded a great sensation of comfort.

'What a splendid hut,' said the Commandant, fanning himself with his cap.

'It's not a hut,' the engineer corrected. 'It is a house. The walls are made of mud. The true hut, entirely made of straw, is now found only among the pygmies.'

The white men continued their conversation on the veranda, where the Chief had had two easy chairs placed for them. Sophie helped me to set up the camp beds we had brought with us. We hung the mosquito nets. When everything was ready I asked the Commandant if he would be needing me for anything else.

'Not for the moment,' he said.

Sophie put the same question word for word to the engineer. Word for word she got the same reply. The engineer was staring at the end of his shoe.

The Chief's attendant was waiting for us. He flicked his fly switch over his shoulders. He told us to follow him.

'You will sleep at the house of my second wife,' he said with great self-satisfaction.

It was a hut with the front specially whitewashed for the Commandant's visit. There were no windows. In the light filtering through the low doorway all that could be seen was an old wash basin in which a hen was sitting on a clutch of eggs.

'This is the house of my second wife,' said the attendant with a broad smile. 'The stream and the wells are on the other side of the courtyard. The lavatory you can smell from here.'

'The elephant does not rot in a secret place,' said Sophie dryly.

'Exactly,' said the attendant as he went off.

When he was almost out of earshot he called out to us. 'You'll be sent food to prepare directly.'

Sophie snapped her fingers and passed her hand over her lips.* Then she made a gesture that seemed to mean 'I take my courage in both hands.' We went into the servants' hut. It was daylight outside and we went into the night. . . .

Sophie bent over the hearth. She pushed the brands together and blew on them several times. At last a flame sprang up. Out of the darkness it revealed a pile of banana bunches on bamboo racks. I was just going to pick one of these when I was seized with a fit of uncontrollable laughter.

'What's the matter now?' said Sophie.

'Nothing . . . you wouldn't understand. . . . I was thinking of Gullet.'

Outside the celebrations were at their height. The white men were watching the bilaba dancers.† The dance is monotonous

* A gesture of astonishment
† A dance in which the torso and the hips are swayed

and they were bored. It was midday. They went into their house. I served them the provisions we had brought from Dangan. When siesta time came they sent the dancers away saying they were too noisy. The dancers went off pretending to be offended. They were covered in dust and sweat.

In the afternoon the Chief came to present in person the chickens, the goat, the basket of eggs and the pawpaws which he intended to sacrifice to the white men. They invited him to take a glass of whisky with them. The Chief was visibly proud to sit among Europeans. Afterwards they all went towards the house where the palavers were conducted.

Evening found the whites broken by the journey and the day's discussions. They hardly touched their evening meal. The Commandant was stretched out across his bed. I knelt down to pull off his boots. A murmured conversation between Sophie and the engineer reached us from the veranda.

I wished the Commandant a good night. As I was going through the door, the engineer who was still sipping his whisky on the veranda, called to me. Night had already fallen. I went towards him, guided by the red glow of his cigarette.

'You are sleeping in the same hut as Sophie, aren't you?' he said.

'Yes . . . Yes, Sir.'

He paused a moment and then went on.

'I'm sending her to the hospital as soon as we get back to Dangan. I'm sending her to the hospital . . .'

He stood up and resumed.

'Sophie was entrusted to me by her father . . . but why am I telling you this? I'm sending her to the hospital . . . and I shall know where to find you again.'

He pulled me by the ear.

'I shall always know where to find you again. . . . You can go now.'

He let me go. Through the darkness I saw his white hands move in a gesture of disgust as if he had touched something unclean.

42

Sophie was waiting for me in the yard. We walked over to our hut in silence. The hen cackled as Sophie pushed open the door. She gathered the brands together and blew on them. A flame flickered and lit up, the inside of the hut. I lay down on one of the bamboo beds. Sophie went over and shut the door. She came and lay down on the other bed. The flame on the hearth died slowly. The edges of our beds disappeared into the darkness. Sophie turned over. The bamboos of the bed creaked.

'It's a long time since I slept in a bamboo bed,' she said. 'It reminds me of my mother ...'

Then she said, 'It's a long time since I slept with a son of the soil in the same hut.'

She yawned.

'Have they cut your tongue out? Aren't you talking to-night?'

'My mouth is tired.'

'What a man you are! Really, I've never come across a man like you. You are shut up all night in a hut with a woman and you say your mouth is tired. When I tell people they won't believe me. They'll say, "Perhaps it's because his knife is not very sharp he prefers to keep it in its sheath".'

'Perhaps,' I said, amused.

'When I tell them, "Yes, he admitted it", they won't believe that either. ... Here, do you know what my boy-friend had to say on the veranda? Are you asleep?'

'No, I'm listening,' I said.

She went on with her monologue.

'First he started calling me names of things to eat. He always does that when he wanted to be mouthing me or when he's moaning, on the job. He calls me "my cabbage" "my chicken". He told me he had brought me with him because he loves me so much. He didn't want to leave me alone in Dangan where I would get bored. He's sly. The truth is he didn't want to leave me alone in Dangan with old Janopoulos. Well he's old enough to be my grandfather, he told me I ought to leave him because he hasn't got any money. Still I prefer my boy-friend to that old toad. He told me he was afraid of the Commandant, his Chief, and that he couldn't tell him he was my my boy-friend. That's why he said I was his cook. I couldn't care less about that. What gets me is why it was a cook he told the Commandant. I wonder why he thought of that. Joseph, do I look like a cook?'

'I don't know, I'm not a white man,' I told her.

'You, you're not like any other men at all. . . . What was he on to you about when he was talking to you on the veranda?'

'Nothing ... nothing much. He told me to look after you ...'

'Ah these whites,' she burst out. 'The dog can die of hunger beside his master's meat. They don't bury the goat up to the horns. They bury him altogether.'

Her voice seemed to be coming from farther and farther away. For a moment I seemed to hear it in a dream. I fell asleep.

* * *

The first goat to come and rub himself against our hut found me already awake. The daylight was filtering through the spaces in the raffia matting on the roof. Outside I could hear the heavy tread of the he-goats going after the females. A cock crowed. ... In the distance, the sound of a bell, or rather a length of railway line ringing. Sophie was still asleep with her face turned to the wall. I got up and thumped her until she woke up. She swore several times before she was properly awake. She smiled weakly and wished me good morning. She pulled down her cloth modestly. In the night it had ridden up to her bottom, uncovering a pair of fine thighs.

I opened the door. The smell of goats came in with the morning freshness and filled the house. Sophie joined me on the veranda.

'They must be still asleep,' she said. 'They were all done up last night ...'

We went up the road to the house where the white men were. Two sets of snores reached us from the veranda. One was thin and tenuous like the croaking of a frog.

'That's my boy-friend,' said Sophie.

The other was deep-toned, like a groan.

'The other must be the Commandant's,' said Sophie again. 'I don't recognize it.'

The Commandant had told me to wake him early. I knocked several times on the door.

'What's that?' called the engineer.

'The Commandant told me to wake him early,' I said.

'All right, all right,' he muttered.

We heard the sharp click of the buckle on a belt. Then the sound of footsteps coming towards the door. The engineer opened it. He smelt of raw meat with other faint indescribable overtones. It was the smell I smelt very morning at the Residence. He rubbed his eyes and tried to smooth back his hair which was all ruffled like a tangle of creepers. He yawned. The gold gleamed in his mouth. He thrust his hands into his pockets and looked first at Sophie, then at me. One moment he was pale and anaemic. The next he had gone a vivid red. He fixed his eyes on mine as if everything else had gone out of his mind. A tic twitched at the corners of his thin mouth. The look on his face was enough to send even a widow at the funeral of her second husband into fits.

'No one can pull faces like Monsieur,' said Sophie, shrieking with laughter.

'Shut up,' the engineer roared, stamping.

The laughter froze on Sophie's face. I felt a tingling at the back of my neck.

'What's going on?' called the Commandant.

'It's the servants,' said the engineer with disgust. He took a few crooked steps on the tips of his toes. His colour went from its red towards green then back to the anaemic pallor.

'We will go back to Dangan this morning,' he said gravely. 'I have had fever in the night.'

'Joseph, start packing. . . . We are leaving this morning,' said the Commandant from inside the hut.

*   *   *

A piece of news so startling it is hard to take it seriously. The Commandant's wife arrives in Yaoundé tomorrow! As the Commandant unfolded the piece of blue paper he went quite red. He leant against the wall as if someone had hit him. He began to talk out loud, disjointedly. Europeans have this way of going red and you can't tell whether they are pleased or not. The cook, the sentry and I did not know what to think.

The Commandant called us in and told us the unexpected news. We showed him how happy we were for his sake. Our laughter and noise – we were clapping our hands as well – took him by surprise. He smiled weakly, then stopped us instantly with a look.

He sent the sentry to get some prisoners to wash the Residence. He told us to get everything into order. He wrote notes for the doctor, the prison-director and Gullet. Then he went off to Yaoundé.

I know now why the Commandant is not like other European men without madams – who send their boys into the location to hire a 'mamie' for them. I wonder what the Commandant's wife will be like. Will she be stocky like the Commandant? Touchy like he is but kind-hearted underneath? I hcpe she is pretty – prettier than all the ladies who come to the European Club. A king should always have the prettiest wife in the kingdom.

*   *   *

She has arrived at last! How pretty she is, how nice. I was the first one to see her. I was just giving the veranda a final sweep when I recognized the sound of my master's car. I didn't say anything to the cook. I rushed over to the sentry who was dozing off. How funny it was to see him wake up with a start and present arms without anyone giving the order.

My master got out of the car. I ran over to open the door for Madame. She smiled at me, I saw her teeth. They were as white as our own girls have. This is very unusual. The Commandant's strong arm was around her wasp-like waist. He told her, 'This is Toundi, my houseboy.' She offered me her hand. It was soft, tiny and limp in my big hand that swallowed it up like a precious jewel. Madame went quite red. Then the Commandant went red too. I got the cases out of the car.

*　　　*　　　*

My happiness has neither day nor night. I didn't know about it, it just burst upon my whole being. I will sing to my flute, I will sing on the banks of rivers, but no words can express my happiness. I have held the hand of my queen. I felt that I was really alive. From now on my hand is sacred and must not know the lower regions of my body. My hand belongs to my queen whose hair is the colour of ebony, with eyes that are like the antelope's, whose skin is pink and white as ivory. A shudder ran through my body at the touch of her tiny moist hand. She trembled like a flower dancing in the breeze. My life was mingling with hers at the touch of her hand. Her smile is refreshing as a spring of water. Her look is as warm as a ray from the setting sun. It bathes you in a light that warms the depths of the heart. I am afraid . . . afraid of myself . . .

*　　　*　　　*

Today Madame made a tour of her new home. She was wearing a pair of black slacks. How they showed off her fine figure. First she visited the kitchen and congratulated the cook on how clean he kept the pots and pans, and also on his *poulet au riz*. The cook was in ecstasies. He went on about his thirty years of experience, and how he had been 'all time very good cookboy'. The laughter went out of Madame's eyes. They became hard. 'Next time put in less pimento,' she said. The cook looked at her, round-eyed.

Next we went to see the goat-park. Madame kept murmuring, 'Ah how sweet they are! How pretty they are!' She let them lick her hands. Then she stopped by the bed of roses and hibiscus. She bent down in front of each flower and breathed its scent in deeply. I was on the other side of the flower-bed facing her. She had forgotten I was there. As I write these words I feel even more unhappy than I felt at Father Gilbert's funeral.

* * *

Madame's first Saturday at Dangan, the European Club was deserted, for the Residence. The whole white world of Dangan was there. Madame was dressed all in white like a newly opened flower. For a while it is the centre and the whole world flutters its wings around it. You could feel that Madame was there. The Commandant moved about with that trace of self-satisfaction that belongs to a man who knows he has married a beautiful wife. He was so elated that when he called me he said 'I say, Joseph,' which he has never done before. What a difference the love and beauty of a woman can make in the heart of a man!

While the men were all admiration in Madame's presence the ladies did not quite manage to conceal under their forced smiles a certain bitterness at being so eclipsed. Mme Salvain was like an oil lamp fetched into the sun. The brightness of Madame's beauty showed up everything which the Good Lord (and he must have been the Devil for Mme Salvain that evening) had forgotten to bring to perfection in all those white ladies which we had once admired in Dangan. The doctor's wife looked as flat as putty flung at a wall. Madame Gullet was stuffed into her slacks like cassava in a banana leaf. The Mesdemoiselles Dubois were alike as a pair of sacks. The wives of the Greeks, usually so talkative, were silent. The American ladies from the Protestant Mission existed only in their bursts of laughter.

For the men, Madame seemed a kind of vision. They had

48

forgotten all the attention they lavished on their wives in the streets of Dangan. There was no attention now except for Madame. Yet among them all there was not one who was able to hold Madame's attention. . . . I had a terrible moment when I saw her eyes linger imperceptibly on the engineer. My eyes met hers over his shoulder. It lasted only a flash. Then she turned her eyes away. I felt myself filled with embarrassment like the day my eyes fell on the Commandant's uncircumcized foreskin.

'Hey, have you gone to sleep?' said the man who disinfects Dangan, showing me his empty glass.

'My God!' he said. 'You'd think he had sleeping sickness.'

All eyes were turned on me.

'Come on, Joseph, come on,' said the Commandant, rapping the table with his lighter.

I pulled the cork out of a bottle of whisky at random and began pouring it into the man's glass. I did not stop till he had called 'Stop, whoa, stop. Holy Christmas!' several times This caused general laughter.

'Man,' said Gullet in a poor imitation of pidgin, 'We no be native drinkers.'

They all laughed again.

'You know,' said Gullet turning his long neck towards Madame and pointing in my direction, 'It's unbelievable the way these chaps can put away the booze . . .'

All the Europeans turned round to look at him. He faltered and pushed back his hair. Then he went on.

'Once . . . once . . . on tour . . .'

He scratched his ear and went red.

'Once I asked a Chief what he would like for a New Year present. Do you know what he said? Absolutely straight. That all the rivers should turn into brandy.'

The doctor slipped the braid up on to his shoulders, emptied his glass and said:

'We're always short of alcohol at the hospital. It's quite frightening. Whatever I do to put a stop to this black market' (the whites sniggered at the phrase) 'in alcohol 90% proof, the orderlies find some way round it.'

Mme Salvain coughed to give herself courage. All heads turned towards her. She seemed to have been forgotten with her husband.

'First thing every morning, it's the smell of alcohol and unwashed body, wafting in from the veranda that tells me my boy has arrived. . . .'

This revelation met with no success. M. Salvain looked up at the ceiling. A silence fell on the whole room.

M. Janopoulos tried to stifle a hiccup with a cough. The other Europeans pretended they had not noticed.

'What a country!' said the wife of the American pastor with a strong accent.

'It's certainly not New York City,' said her plump companion, fatuously.

The other whites pretended not to understand. The two of them laughed together as if they were alone.

'There are no morals at all in this country,' groaned the doctor's wife, trying to sound as if she were in despair.

'Nor in Paris for that matter,' came back the schoolmaster.

The remark ran through the bodies of the Europeans in the room like an electric current. They shuddered, one by one. The doctor's ears grew blood-red. Only Madame remained unmoved, and the American ladies who had been so busy whispering among themselves that they had heard nothing. The man who disinfects Dangan was breathing heavily. He turned sharply to the schoolmaster.

'What . . . what do you . . . what do you mean by that?' he stammered.

The schoolmaster made a little grimace of contempt and shrugged his shoulders. The other man rose and walked over to him. The schoolmaster watched without concern. Was the disinfector going to fly at his throat? The moment was tense.

'You nasty little rabble rouser,' he snapped.

'Please, please, M. Fernand,' said the Commandant, coming between them.

M. Fernand went back to his seat and was about to sit down. As his behind touched the bottom of the armchair he seemed to collapse as if he had been bitten by a scorpion. Once or twice his arms thrashed the air. He opened his mouth, shut it, then ran his tongue over his lips.

'You're a traitor, M. Salvain,' he said, 'a traitor. Ever since you came to this country you have behaved in a way unworthy of a Frenchman. You're stirring the natives up against us. You keep telling them that they are as good as we are – as if they hadn't got a high enough opinion of themselves already ...'

M. Fernand sat down. Gullet nodded his head at the end of his neck in approval. Other heads followed this lead. Madame's head remained still.

'Poor France,' said Gullet, blowing his nose.

The schoolmaster shrugged. Madame looked up at the ceiling. The doctor's wife murmured something into her husband's ear. She joined her hands, smirked, then turned towards Madame and began in a strange voice.

'My dear, did you go and see the Japanese ballet at the *Théâtre Marigny*?'

'I didn't have time. I was too busy running from one office to the next so as to be here in time to surprise Robert on his birthday.'

She gazed fondly at her husband, who caressed her arm. The doctor's wife returned to the attack. She mentioned a newspaper that had praised the Japanese ballet. When she had run out of things to say, one of the Mesdemoiselles Dubois took over. She mentioned the names of several white men who I suppose must have been musicians or had something to do with music. She was very sorry she had not had Madame's opportunity of being in Paris at the beginning of the week. She lamented that the tennis courts had already turned to mud in the first rains and that she had not found anyone who could play

51

really well at Dangan. Mme Salvain spoke of horses, complaining that the tsetse fly of the forest zone had made it impossible for the Africans to rear them. The engineer said something could perhaps be done. . . . M. Janopoulos discussed the price of cocoa with the Commandant. The doctor expressed the desire to have a European midwife. The schoolmaster spoke with authority. He tried to explain African behaviour. Everybody told his own little African story to refute him and demonstrate that the African is a child or a fool. . . .

They were sorry Father Vandermayer was not present, a saintly man, devoting his life to ungrateful savages. They lamented 'the Martyr' as they called Father Gilbert because he died on African soil. The doctor's wife, with tears in her voice, promised to take Madame to lay flowers on his grave.

'He was somebody, he was,' said M. Fernand so that M. Salvain could hear.

The Americans had forgotten everyone else and were now talking in their own language.

When a glass was empty I rushed to fill it up. Then I came straight back to my place between the leaf of the door and the refrigerator. The engineer had his back to me. Madame and the Commandant were facing me. Madame was not drinking spirits. The wives of the Greeks were chatting quietly with their husbands. Their laughter came seldom like the tears of a dog.

The conversation came round to the natives again.

'Poor France,' said Gullet again. 'Natives are now Ministers in Paris!'

What was the Republic coming to? Each of the Europeans present found his own reason for asking the question.

M. Fernand was the first to voice it.

'What is the world coming to?' echoed Gullet.

Then they talked about the need for a *coup d'état* to regenerate France. They spoke of their kings, about someone called Napoleon. . . . Everyone was astonished when Madame said that the step-father of an Empress they called Josephine was a Negro.

So they talked about natives again ... the Yellow Peril hadn't been averted yet, and here was the Black Peril already looming up.... What would happen to civilization? ...

The first drops of rain rattled on the corrugated-iron roof of the Residence. The doctor and his wife were the first to rise to their feet. The others followed. They slithered about the floor as if they were on a banana skin. The Commandant when addressed merely grunted and left Madame to lead the guests out on to the veranda by herself. The cars moved off. Madame waited until the last red light had disappeared into the night.

*   *   *

I went with Madame to Dangan market; she insisted on going herself and doing her own shopping. She was wearing her black slacks that show off her figure and a large straw hat that she brought with her from Paris. The market place of Dangan is about five minutes from the Residence. It is a yard with sheds along two sides. In one of these there is a butchery and in the other a shop for fish. There is a stream full of rubbish used as a dustbin and sometimes for bathing.

This is the most lively place in Dangan, especially on Saturday mornings. It is a meeting place for all the natives from the location and from the villages. We went on foot. I carried Madame's shopping basket. She tripped along in front of me, lithe and graceful as a gazelle. When we were a dozen yards away the Africans removed their hats. Without showing they were addressing me they called out in our language if this was really *her*. I nodded.

'I'm glad I've met her before I go to confession,' one of them said.

'If she had been the one to pour ointment on our Lord's feet, the Bible story would have been rather different,' said someone else.

'Very different!' said a third.

The catechists followed us with their eyes. A young man sped past on his bicycle.

'Now there's a woman,' he shouted, 'a woman among women.'

Comments came flying from all sides. The men saluted us and then stayed frozen in their attitudes.

'See the way those buttocks go!' someone said. 'What a figure, what hair.'

'What couldn't I do with what's inside those slacks,' said someone else longingly.

'Man, your shorts must be soaked,' a third shouted at me.

'What a shame it's all reserved for the uncircumcized,' came yet another, pulling a face to show his vexation.

The women admired in silence. They passed the palms of their hands over their lips. One of them said she thought Madame's buttocks were too soft.

M. Janopoulos appeared from somewhere and offered Madame a lift in his powerful American car. She said she wanted to explore Dangan on foot. The Greek gave me a brief glance over Madame's shoulder. She blushed. He roared off.

At the market, the crowd opened up in front of us of its own accord. Madame bought pineapples, oranges and a few bananas. She went to the fish stall. One of the Africans was satisfying an urgent need into the edge of the stream. Madame did not blush.

At ten o'clock we took the road back to the Residence.

Suddenly she asked me 'Boy, what are these people saying?'

'Nothing . . .' I said embarrassed.

'What do you mean, nothing?' she said, turning round. 'All the jabbering everywhere I go must mean something.'

'They think you're . . . you're very pretty,' I said, breathless.

I shall never forget the look she gave me as I brought out these words. Her eyes grew small and an expression I cannot describe came over her face. She had gone red again. I felt a prickly heat over me from the nape of my neck down to the soles of my feet. Madame did her best to smile.

'That is very nice of them,' she said. 'But why all the secrecy? Why are you looking so stupid?'

The rest of the way home she did not speak.

* * *

Madame was swinging in a hammock with a book in her hand. While I was bringing her something to drink she asked me:

'Boy, why don't you like working at the Residence?'

I stood disconcerted, my mouth open. She went on:

'You look as if you find it a drudgery. Oh of course we are very satisfied with you. ... You have no faults, you are always punctual, you are a conscientious worker ... but you haven't got that joy one finds in African workers. ... You give the impression that you are doing a houseboy's job while waiting for something else to come along.'

Madame spoke without a pause, looking straight ahead. She turned towards me.

'What does your father do?'

'He is dead.'

'I'm sorry ...'

'Madame is very kind.'

After a pause she went on:

'What did he do when he was alive?'

'He set porcupine traps.'

'How funny.' She laughed. 'And can you set porcupine traps as well?'

'Yes, Madame.'

She swayed back and forth in the hammock and tapped the ash from the cigarette she was contentedly puffing. She blew smoke out of her mouth and nose into the space that separated us. She picked off a tiny piece of paper stuck to her lower lip and blew it towards me.

'You see,' she went on. 'You've already got as far as being the Commandant's houseboy.'

She gave me a smile which curled her upper lip. Her eyes gleamed. They seemed to be trying to make some discovery in my face. To cover up, she emptied her glass and said:

'Are you married?'

'No, madame.'

'Yet you earn enough to be able to buy a wife. ... Robert says that as the Commandant's houseboy you would be a good match. ... You must start a family.'

She smiled.

'A family, a big family, eh?'

'Perhaps, Madame, but my wife and children will never be able to eat and dress like Madame or like white children.'

'Oh dear,' she laughed. 'You are getting big ideas.'

She went on. 'You must be serious. Everyone has their position in life. You are a houseboy, my husband is Commandant ... nothing can be done about it. You are a Christian, aren't you?'

'Yes, Madame, more or less.'

'What do you mean "more or less"?'

'Not very Christian, Madame. Christian because the priest poured water on my head and gave me a European name.'

'I can hardly credit what you are telling me now. The Commandant told me you were a very firm believer.'

'We have to believe the white man's stories – more or less.'

'So that's the way it is, is it?'

I had taken her breath away.

'But,' she went on, 'don't you believe in God any more? Have you gone back to being a pagan?'

'The river does not go back to its spring ... I think there is a proverb like that in Madame's country too.'

'Yes indeed ... Well, it's all very interesting,' she said, amused. 'Now get my shower ready. How hot it gets!'

*　　*　　*

We have never sat up so late in the location as we did last night. All the Africans had gathered round a fire in the hut we used for discussions.

When I came in, the small group of elders was listening to Ali the Hausa man. He is the only travelling merchant in the location. His goatee beard is white and he is so wise he has been given a place among the elders of Dangan. He was interrupted by Mekongo, the army veteran.

'I tell you you are wasting your time over the Commandant's wife. You have never slept with a white woman so you are wasting your time. I've fought in the white man's country. I've left a leg there and I've no regrets. I've seen all kinds of white women and I think that I can say that the Commandant's wife is a white woman among white women.'

'You've been to the war,' said someone to him, 'you've slept with white women. Tell us if white women are better than ours. It is not a foolish question to ask. Why do the whites forbid us their women?'

'Perhaps it's because they are uncircumcized and we are not,' someone else suggested.

Everyone burst into laughter. When it became quiet again Mekongo answered the man who had asked the question.

'Obila, you have a head and it is full of wisdom. The question you ask is a wise man's question, the question of a wise man who is seeking to understand. Our ancestors said, "Truth lies beyond the mountains. You must travel to find it." I have travelled. I have made the great journey you know of. I have slept with white women. I have made war. I have lost my leg and I can answer your question.

'When I left this country I was already a man. If I had been a child the white men would not have called me. When I went to the war I left a woman with child. During the whole of the fighting in Libya I did not think about women. After our victory, my battalion was posted to Algiers. We had twenty days leave. I had all my pay. I could break the sixth commandment. Death was far away. My comrades were white men, real white men. They said to me, "Friend, you come with us. Many-many women in town." I asked them "Black women?" They told me, "White women, white madams." I did not know whites and blacks could sleep together. But when my white friends told me that the Saras already had white mistresses I decided to go with them. They took me to a brothel. That is a big house, full of women. In all my life I had never seen such a thing. Women of all colours, all sizes, all ages. Some had hair like the beard on a maize cob, others had hair blacker than tar or redder than the laterite of our houses. A white man with a great belly and bags under his eyes told me to choose one of the women who were filing in front of me. I chose a real white woman with hair the colour of the beard on a corn cob, eyes like a panther, buttocks like putty stuck on the wall.'

'Ah, a real white woman,' said someone in approval.

Everyone nodded. A murmur of approval ran through the crowd. Mekongo went on:

'When I had chosen, the woman came up to me and put her hand under my chin. We went into a room. I had never seen such a room. There were mirrors everywhere. Images of us covered the walls and the ceiling. There was a great bed made in the white man's style. Beyond it there was a screen and behind the screen everything necessary for washing. The woman I had chosen was wearing a long dress with many buttons in front. She was as tall as I was and as white as a tick-bird. Her hair the colour of the maize beard fell down on to her shoulders. She came close to me and laughed and called me "My little chick". My heart seemed to stop beating. I stood up. She backed away, frightened. I asked her why she had insulted me. She began to laugh and to twist her body. I would have struck her but I was afraid they would throw me out. When we had calmed down she told me she had not insulted me and that white women call the men that go with them all sorts of names. She showed me a letter she was going to send to one of her lieutenant-chicks. There, sure enough, I read "my adorable chick" or some such phrase. So I knew she was telling the truth.'

'What happened next was ... but I want the children sent away first.'

The children were sent out and went off whining.

'I think they have all gone now,' said Mekongo. 'Come closer, I do not want to raise my voice. I am going to talk about things which are not talked about ...'

The men gathered closely around Mekongo.

'You were lucky to go to the war,' someone said.

Then I came away.

* * *

The master has been away on tour for two weeks now. Madame seemed nervous all the afternoon. She asked me several times if anyone had called. She had the sentry in and asked him the same question. I wonder who she could be expecting.

Then she began to pace up and down on the veranda. Madame is growing bored.

* * *

The laundryman I found for Madame is an intelligent lad. He is younger than I am and he doesn't speak French very well. He used to work at the hospital. He told me he did all kinds of jobs there. Sometimes he helped the labourers to weed the court-yard, sometimes he emptied the dustbins where they throw the old bandages. He also helped the orderlies to hold the feet of difficult patients who did not want to be treated in the hospital and who had been brought by force in the ambulance.

I asked him what he thought of Madame.

'Like all the white women round here,' he said.

'But the prettiest,' I insisted.

'You know,' he said, shrugging his shoulders, 'I don't know

how you tell whether a white woman is pretty or not.'

He's a strange lad . . . His name is Baklu.

I wonder who Madame could have been expecting yesterday.

*   *   *

The prison-director came to have a chat with Madame. I wonder if he was the one she was expecting the other day . . .

*   *   *

It was him, it was M. Moreau that Madame was expecting the other day. Why didn't I think of him? Of all the whites in Dangan, M. Moreau is the one who is really a man among men. The Africans call him 'The White Elephant'. He's the kind of man you can't help remembering once you've seen him. Those broad shoulders stick in the mind. Everyone in Dangan feels a certain respect, even the Commandant.

I wonder why he didn't come with the others to welcome Madame. Has the Lion waited till the shepherd has gone before coming to devour his ewe?

The sentry came to me this morning on tiptoe with his big finger on his lips. Madame was still asleep. He laid his arms on my shoulders and I felt his wet lips at my ear. I had no idea what the secrecy could be about.

'The truth is,' he said under his breath, 'can I deny that I saw the prison-director leaving Madame after midnight?'

The sentry took me by the hand and drew me to the edge of the veranda.

'Things are as they are,' he went on mysteriously, 'and someone is to blame for them and they go the way they have to go. If I talk it is because I have a mouth. If I see, it is because I have eyes. The eye goes farther and faster than the mouth, nothing stops it . . .

'So I'm talking,' he said after a pause.

He passed his big hand over his lips.

'I'm talking and what I'm saying is the panther is prowling around the sheep. It's not me, it's these' (he pointed his two index fingers towards his eyes) 'that saw it.'

The sentry watched me as if he were expecting something.

'You're lucky to be able to sweat in this cold weather,' he said. 'I can see you've still got young blood.'

Without thinking I brought my hand up to my nose. It was damp. I sat down on the steps. I felt filled with a strange numbness. My legs seemed to have disappeared.

'You might have told me instead of getting drunk by yourself,' said the sentry sitting down heavily beside me. 'You might have brought me something to warm my belly.'

He yawned.

'Did you hear them talking all night?' I heard myself asking him.

'Who?' said the sentry, puzzled.

'What do you mean, "Who"?' I said angrily, 'Madame and . . .'

'Aaaaaaaaaaakiaaaaay!' he shouted. It always starts like that, with questions that don't end. I don't understand you, you youngsters today. In the time of the Germans we took no interest in the affairs of the whites. I don't understand. I don't understand why you should ask me such a question . . .'

He sighed.

'I didn't tell you I heard them . . . I told you that what they said came into my ears. I didn't do anything . . .'

'Good morning, friends. Have you slept well?'

It was Baklu who had just arrived. He found a place and sat down between the sentry and me. The sentry muttered something.

'You're looking glum, the two of you,' said Baklu.

He looked at us, one after the other. The constable began to get up. Baklu held him by the bottom of his shorts. He dropped back, resigned.

'It's all my fault,' said the sentry with a little quaver in his voice. 'My mouth is always running away with me . . .'

He pressed his lips together.

'I was there and without wanting to, I saw and heard.'

'You talk as if you had a scorpion hanging on to your balls,' said Baklu. 'You needn't be afraid with me. My ear is a tomb. You won't refuse to tell a friend,' he begged, 'a real friend...'

'I know, I know,' said the sentry, swaying his head from side to side.

He spread his hands like a priest saying 'Dominus vobiscum.' He began:

'This is what has upset me. I told Toundi what came into my ears and what happened in front of my eyes ... The White Elephant you know of visited the Commandant's field while he was away ...'

'What business of yours is that?' Baklu asked, puzzled.

'None at all. That's exactly what I was saying to Toundi...'

Baklu turned to me. He looked at me intently for a long time. Then he turned away his eyes. He pulled a face of annoyance, scratched his head and coughed.

'Toundi, my brother, my dear brother, if you knew how you worry me.... What are you after? Since when does the pot rub itself against the hammer? What do you want?'

'Now you are talking like one of the elders,' said the sentry, approving loudly. 'It is good to know that not all the young men today are fools....'

The bugle at the police camp sounded eight o'clock.

'To work,' said Baklu getting to his feet. 'We are here to work and only to work.'

'Yet it makes me feel sick to think that Madame could do that to the Commandant,' said the sentry. 'And she's only just come from France.'

'Try to keep your big mouth shut,' Baklu told him. 'We've agreed that this business has nothing to do with us. Yet you go on talking about it.'

'My son,' said the sentry, 'you know there is nothing worse

than thoughts. It's nothing to do with me ... only I want to know whether it's happened already or hasn't happened yet. ... You're the laundryman, you can have a look at the sheets.'

'Now that is an idea which would not have occurred to me,' said Baklu. 'You are an old tortoise.'

They laughed and winked at each other. I went off to get Madame's shower ready.

Baklu was waiting outside the washhouse. At nine o'clock Madame was still not up. The sentry came over and joined Baklu. I heard scraps of their conversation. The question was to find out whether it had happened or not. A thousand thoughts rushed into my mind. I used to wonder, before this, how Madame, being so feminine, could be altogether satisfied with the Master. ... The prison-director isn't the kind of man who goes courting. He knows what he wants. He's not the man to wait for the fruit to drop off the tree.

AFTERNOON

It is all over. Poor Commandant.

Eleven o'clock Madame was still sleeping. I knew by then that something was wrong. Just before twelve she called the laundryman. From the kitchen I saw Baklu, chuckling to himself, slip by to the washhouse. He made signs to the sentry who burst into laughter. Then he signalled me to follow him. I ran to pour the pan of hot water into the bath, then I joined Baklu and the sentry in the washhouse.

There is no doubt. It took place during the night. ... Poor Commandant!

M. Moreau came back at four o'clock. Madame was full of happiness. She sang and skipped about the house like a young kid.

Poor Commandant!

* * *

One of the constables who was with my master on tour came to the Residence at midday. He brought a letter for Madame.

She glanced through it, wrote something on the back and put it into another envelope which I took right away to the prison-director.

When M. Moreau saw me, he got up from the table where he was having lunch with his wife and met me on the veranda. He almost snatched the letter from my hands. When he had read it I thought he was going to fling his arms around me. He gave me a packet of cigarettes. That was all I had to tell Madame for an answer. She seemed delighted as well.

These whites, once their passions get a hold, nothing else matters to them.

It will take the master several more days before he is finished in the forest of the 'Evil Chimpanzee'.

Poor master . . .

* * *

Madame sent all the staff off at six o'clock. She told me to stay to serve dinner. M. and Mme Moreau were coming. They arrived at seven o'clock. Madame wore her tightly fitting black silk dress. M. Moreau resplendent in a dark tailored suit. Mme Moreau looked insignificant. She was in a white dress which did not at all emphasize her breasts or hips. I wonder how a woman who is so fragile can carry a strapping giant like the director. As they arrived at the Residence, I knew it was to be a martyrdom for Mme Moreau. To invite them at all seemed to me very daring.

My mistress and M. Moreau hardly bothered about pretences. They kept their hands under the table. It did not take much to guess what was going on. Mme Moreau got up at the first opportunity and asked me to show her the way to the toilet. I went in front on to the veranda with an electric torch. Mme Moreau came behind, sniffing. She was holding a handkerchief to her mouth.

I left her at the toilet and crept back. There was a crack in the drawing-room window through which the light was shining. I peered in. M. Moreau was kissing Madame on the mouth. I stole back to wait for Mme Moreau. She seemed to be taking a long time. Half an hour had gone by when we went back into the room. Mme Moreau powdered herself and then saying she had a violent headache she asked Madame and her husband to excuse her. M. Moreau took her home in the car.

An hour later he was back.

'You may go, Joseph,' said Madame primly.

* * *

My master came back this morning. It is not a good sign that he should come so unexpectedly. The sentry says he must have had a dream that someone was sleeping with his wife.

I was washing up when the familiar sound of the engine came to a stop just by the garage. It was eleven o'clock and Madame who has not been getting up till noon since her husband went away was still basking in her night of love.

I ran out to the garage to take my master's luggage.

'Ah, hallo, Joseph. Isn't Madame in?'

'Yes, Sir. She is still in bed.'

'Is she ill?'

'I don't know, Sir.'

My master hurried towards the Residence, his stubby legs working backwards and forwards busily. I came up behind him on my long legs, carrying his bag on my head. I felt sorry for this man, so anxiously running towards a wife who no longer cared for him alone. I wanted to see how Madame would behave with her husband home now she had deceived him. She was waiting for the Commandant on the veranda, wrapped in her bath-robe. She gave a pale smile and went towards him. My master kissed her on the mouth. This time she did not shut her eyes.

I stood behind them. I could not ask them to make way for me to carry the master's bag into his room. .... I lowered my eyes. For a fraction of a second I raised them and they met Madame's eyes. I saw them grow small, then large as if she could see something that astonished her. Instinctively I looked down at my feet to make sure I wasn't standing beside a poisonous snake. I heard my master asking Madame what was wrong.

'But you look quite ill, Suzy.'

'Oh, it's nothing,' she said.

My master still had his back to me. Madame's eyes never left me. The Commandant released her from his arms and they went inside.

I stood for a few moments at the foot of the steps rooted to the spot by the look in Madame's eyes. I ferreted about the stems of the citronellas, a favourite place for the little deadly poisonous green snakes. I felt something soft and sticky under my feet. With a shriek I leapt into the air. My master rushed to the window. I was ashamed at myself, ashamed because I had shrieked when I felt a banana skin with the sole of my foot.

'What's the matter, Joseph?' called the Commandant.

'Nothing, sir.'

'Come on, you don't go round howling at the top of your voice for no reason at all. Or is this some custom on your part of the world?'

'Yes, sir.' I seized on the hint. 'It is to greet your arrival.'

As I spoke I put on my most naïve grin. The Commandant shrugged his shoulders and disappeared. I went into the drawing-room and asked for the key to the bedroom so that I could unpack his bag.

'Put it on the chair,' said Madame. 'I'll unpack it myself.'

Lunch was gloomy. An oppressive silence filled the whole house. I stood quietly by the refrigerator. The Commandant had his back to me. Madame kept her head bent over her plate.

Before my master went away the meals had always been very cheerful, with Madame's gay chatter running on.

The Commandant asked his wife again if she were ill.

'I tell you I'm perfectly all right,' she said.

'I don't understand ... I don't understand,' muttered the Commandant. 'Perhaps the heat is affecting your nerves. You must see a doctor. Are you sure you haven't got a headache?'

'Yes, a little,' said Madame. She sounded remote.

'Boy, bring some aspirin,' ordered my master.

When I gave the box to Madame her hand was trembling.

'You see you'll feel better,' said the Commandant. 'But you must see a doctor tomorrow.'

Clumsily he moved towards the veranda.

Second
Exercise Book

In Dangan the European quarter and the African quarter are quite separate. But what goes on underneath those corrugated-iron roofs is known down to the smallest detail inside the mud-walled huts. The eyes that live in the native location strip the whites naked. The whites on the other hand go about blind. There was not a soul unaware that the wife of the Commandant was deceiving her husband with M. Moreau the prison-director and our greatest terror.

'None of these white women are much good,' M. Moreau's houseboy said to me the other day. 'Even the wife of a great chief like the Commandant lets herself be taken on the seat of her husband's car down some Dangan lane. It wouldn't matter but the next thing is they're shooting each other over this kind of business.'

Then he told me how he had seen two white men in Spanish Guinea kill each other over a woman who wasn't even completely white, one of the women even we look down on ... How can anyone kill or get himself killed over a woman? Our ancestors were wise when they said, 'A woman is a cob of maize for any mouth that has its teeth.'

* * *

For the first time Madame had a visit from her lover while her husband was here. M. Moreau at the Residence; my stomach was uneasy all the evening and now I am furious with myself. How can I get rid of this ridiculous sentimentality which makes me suffer over matters which have nothing whatever to do with me?

These Europeans certainly take chances when their

emotions are involved. I hardly expected M. Moreau to come to the Residence now the whole of Dangan knows about him. But the Commandant is too convinced of his own importance to suspect his wife. He spent the evening stuffing himself like a turkey, quite unaware of those little superfluous attentions that Madame was lavishing on him like a woman whose conscience was not clear. Nor did he notice the icy politeness between Madame and their guest, the politeness of accomplices pretending not to know each other.

It is interesting how many expressions follow, one after the other, across a woman's face at times like these. Madame had one set of little smiles for her lover and a completely different set for her husband. When she smiled at M. Moreau I could see only her eyelashes. When she smiled at the Commandant you could tell from the perspiration on her forehead how hard she was trying to keep her laughter sounding completely natural. Dabbing away an imaginary tear, she just managed ... The Commandant gave a little supercilious laugh, followed by an expression of irritation as if he were vexed that the prison-director had not noticed how condescending he was being. Then the director gave a tentative laugh and this in turn brought some laughter from Madame. This time it was quite genuine.

Madame's eyes happened to wander in the direction of the refrigerator where I was standing to await my orders. She went red and immediately changed the conversation to the subject of Africans. M. Moreau talked about those he had in prison. From the way he talked you would have gathered that Dangan prison was a kind of African paradise and that those who came out feet first had died of sheer delight ... Ah, these whites ...

* * *

Madame was waiting for me on the steps. When she saw me she stopped walking up and down. She kept her eyes on me as I came up.

'I've been waiting for half an hour,' she said, controlling her impatience. 'Why did you go off like that at midday? I thought your day finished at midnight. Where have you been?'

'In the sun, Madame,' I said, giving my silliest smile.

That made things worse.

'Are you making fun of me?'

'N . . . nn . . . no Madame,' I said, putting on a stammer.

'You think you're very clever,' she said with a scornful smile, 'For some time now you've begun to think you can do what you like. Everyone has noticed it, even the guests!'

She thrust her hands into the pockets of her silk dressing-down. Her eyes grew small. She came towards me. A light breeze from behind her brought a smell of perfume and female sweat that seemed to scorch my body. She looked at me, disconcerted. She passed her hand over her face and went on calmly.

'From now on, the very first sign of trouble from you and you're dismissed. You can go now.'

I slipped off to the kitchen. It was time for the washing-up. From the kitchen I saw Madame put on her topee and go out to inspect Baklu's washing hanging in the yard.

'Washman, washman,' she called.

No reply. She sprang into the washhouse like a wounded panther. I knew Baklu went to sleep there through the afternoon waiting for his washing to dry in the sun. If you listened carefully you could hear his snores from the kitchen. There came the sound of a raised voice.

'Baklu in trouble,' said the cook.

'Idle creature! You lazy idle loafer!' shrieked Madame. 'Where do you think you are . . . where do any of you think you are? His lordship takes his ease . . . Go on, out you get!'

Baklu, only half awake, came lurching across the yard followed by Madame. For a moment she hesitated in her pursuit of the huge craggy frame fluttering in its worn-out doorman's uniform, and Baklu stopped, rubbing his eyes and suppressing a yawn. Madame's vociferations seemed gradually to make him aware of her presence. Then full realization dawned . . . he had the Commandant's wife on his heels. He began to move on in some alarm. They both came up to where the washing line was stretched across.

'You call that clean?' shouted Madame, seizing pairs of the Commandant's underpants and vests and flinging them at Baklu's head. 'You loafer.'

The Commandant's khaki shorts, Madame's chemises, her slips, the sheets, all came flying at his head. He was intoning his excuses and Madame, her lower lip stuck out and pulling a strange face, mimicked him, rocking her head from side to side.

'They won't come like new, they won't come like new . . .'

Baklu was picking up the washing all around him. Madame seemed not to hear him. She went on and on. I had never seen her like this before.

'What can one expect from any of you!' she said. 'And when people who really knew what they were talking about told me, I didn't believe them! . . . Well, there's going to be a change . . .'

'The prison-director knew what he was talking about when he said what you needed was the big stick,' she went on. 'Well, that's what you're going to get, that's what you're going to get. We shall see who wins in the end.'

She looked towards the kitchen and saw us at the window. Then it was our turn. She carried out an inspection and found a broken decanter. She fixed a price and deducted it from the cook's wages and mine. It came to half our month's earnings.

'And that's only a beginning,' she said, 'only a beginning.'

She went on talking for a long while standing in the doorway of the kitchen. She called the cook an old baboon. She loured. Then finding she could think of nothing else to say, she ran back to the Residence. The door of the drawing-room was slammed. Later we heard the noise of the truck being driven out of the garage. The sentry ran round to join us in the kitchen. He waved his huge arms about, doubling up with laughter. He stole a quick glance back towards the Residence to reassure himself.

'She's gone,' he said, 'today's Thursday.' He smiled knowingly.

'I hadn't thought of that,' said Baklu. 'Anyway she's ready for it. Lucky director. Madame is really ready.'

'Did you see under her armpits?' added the sentry. 'It was coming down like rain. She was ready for it all right!'

The cook was bent over cleaning some beans. He wiped his hand across his face.

'I shall never save up enough to buy a wife,' he said. 'There's not enough left now to buy cigarettes . . .'

'Fancy being at the mercy of a bitch like that,' said the sentry sadly.

We were silent.

'Fancy . . .' I heard myself repeating.

*　　*　　*

My master is off into the bush again this morning. He is indefatigable. I am frightened. It makes things very awkward for me. While he was here I had some security. What has Madame got up her sleeve? She says nothing. She won't even call me by name. She just signals. She signalled me to come this morning when she gave me the letter. I had to take it to her lover as soon as her husband had gone.

The prison-director was busy with two Africans suspected of stealing from M. Janopoulos. He was 'teaching them how to behave'.

With the help of a constable he was giving them a flogging in front of M. Janopoulos. They were stripped to the waist and handcuffed. There was a rope round their necks, tied to the pole in the Flogging Yard, so that they couldn't turn their necks towards the blows.

It was terrible. The hippopotamus-hide whip tore up their flesh. Every time they groaned it went through my bowels.

M. Moreau with his hair down over his face and his shirt sleeves rolled up was setting about them so violently that I wondered, in agony of mind, if they would come out of it alive. Chewing on his cigar M. Janopoulos released his dog. It mouthed about the heels of the prisoners and tore at their trousers.

'Confess, you thieves,' shouted M. Moreau. 'Give them the butt of your rifle, Ndjangoula.'

The huge Sara ran up, presented his weapon and brought down the butt on the suspects.

'Not on the head, Ndjangoula, they've got hard heads. In the kidneys.'

Ndjangoula brought the butt down on their kidneys. They went down, got up and then went down again under another violent blow to the kidneys.

Janopoulos was laughing. M. Moreau panted for breath. The prisoners had lost consciousness.

M. Moreau is right, we must have hard heads. When Ndjangoula brought down his rifle butt the first time, I thought their skulls would shatter. I could not hold myself from shaking as I watched. It was terrible. I thought of all the priests, all the pastors, all the white men, who come to save our souls and preach love of our neighbours. Is the white man's neighbour only other white men? Who can go on believing the stuff we are served up in the churches when things happen like I saw today . . .

It will be the usual thing. M. Moreau's suspects will be sent to the 'Blackman's Grave' where they will spend a few days painfully dying. Then they will be buried naked in the prisoners' cemetery. On Sunday, the priest will say, 'Dearly beloved brethren, pray for all those prisoners who die without making their peace with God.' M. Moreau will present his upturned topee to the faithful. Everyone will put in a little more than he had intended. All the money goes to the whites. They are always thinking up new ways to get back what little money they pay us.

How wretched we are.

I can't remember what I did when I got back to the Residence, I was so upset by what I had seen. There are some things it is better never to see. Once you have seen them, you can never stop living through them over and over again.

I don't think I shall ever forget what I have seen. I shall never forget that guttural, inhuman cry from the smaller of the two suspects when Ndjangoula brought the butt down on him with such force that even M. Moreau swore under his breath and M. Janopoulos dropped his cigar. The whites went off, shrugging and gesticulating. M. Moreau turned round suddenly and beckoned to me. He grabbed me by the shoulder. Janopoulos exchanged glances with him. I could feel his hand through my jersey, burning and damp. When we were out of sight of M. Janopoulos, M. Moreau took his hand from my shoulder and began to feel in his pockets. He offered me a cigarette and lit up himself.

'Don't you smoke?' he said, offering me a light.

'Not in the daytime,' I said, not knowing what to say.

He shrugged and took a long draw at his cigarette.

'Tell Madame I'll be over at . . . let me see' (he looked at his watch) 'um . . . um . . . I'll be over at three o'clock. All right?'

'Yes, Sir, yes, Sir,' I said.

He held me by the back of my neck and made me look at him. The cigarette I had put behind my ear fell down. I tried to bend down and pick it up so I would not have to look at him. He put his foot on the cigarette and I felt his fingers tighten on my neck.

'No tricks with me, eh?' he said, under his breath, forcing me to stand upright.

'Listen, my lad,' he said, 'those chaps in there . . . they know me . . . See?' He pointed his thumb over his shoulder towards the prison. Then he smiled and tossed me the packet of cigarettes. His movement was so unexpected that I missed my catch. The packet flew over my head.

'Pick it up . . . it's for you,' he said, laughing. 'You play along with me, you get things given you. You're a friend of mine, aren't you?'

'Yes, Sir,' I heard myself say.

'Good,' he said. 'You remember what I told you?'

'Yes, Sir.'

'What did I tell you?'

'You said you were coming to see Madame at three o'clock.'

'Good ... Don't forget to tell her ... When is the Commandant coming back?'

'I don't know, Sir.'

'Good. Off you go,' he said, tossing me a five-franc note.

He turned and went away.

When I got back to the Residence I found my hand had torn the note to pieces.

Madame was watching for me to come back, pretending to be busy with the flowers. She came up to where I was. Then her smile froze. She went red. She tried to look me back in the eye but turned away. She slapped at an imaginary fly on her leg.

'He will come at three ... at siesta time,' I said moving off.

Her lips moved. Her breasts were going up and down like a bellows. Her colour became ashen. She cupped her chin in her left hand, smoothing her dress with the other.

When I joined the cook he said to me:

'You're going to be in trouble, talking to Madame all the time with a smile at the corner of your mouth ... Didn't you hear how she said, "Thank you, Monsieur Toundi". It's a bad sign when a white starts being polite to a native ...'

M. Moreau was there well before three o'clock. Madame was waiting for him, swinging in her hammock. He had changed his shirt. Over the khaki shorts he had been wearing in the morning he wore a big coloured shirt rather like a Hausa's boubou. He did not come by the usual path, the one he had worn himself coming on moonlight nights when the Commandant was away. This path emerged directly underneath Madame's window. We wondered why he had taken the main road instead where he could be seen from the doctor's house just below the Residence. He came along swinging a little chain around his fingers. When Madame saw him coming she called me and told me to bring two whiskies. Madame always drinks spirits when her husband is away. She jumped out of the hammock and offered the prison-director her arm. It was bare to the shoulder and he kept his lips pressed to it for a long while. He was confident and expectant. Madame twisted herself away, standing up on her toes. They both laughed and went into the drawing-room together. Madame sat down on the sofa and indicated to the prison-director the place beside her. I drew up a small table on which I had placed the two whiskies.

'He's a funny chap, your boy,' said M. Moreau as I was going away.

'He's Mon-sieur Toun-di,' said Madame stressing each syllable.

'How long has he been with you?' asked M. Moreau.

'Robert took him on,' said Madame. 'It seems he was Father Gilbert's boy. Father Gilbert's successor spoke very well of him ... He rather fancies himself. He has ideas about his own importance. Just lately he has been taking liberties. But he knows now how far he can go.'

M. Moreau raised himself and stubbed out his cigarette in the ashtray. While Madame was talking he rolled his eyes, opened them wide, shut them and opened them again with great sweeps of his eyebrows. He gave me a dangerous look. A lock of hair hanging down over his forehead trembled. He rubbed his hands and leant towards Madame. At the same time he kept his eyes on me.

'Come here,' said the prison-director, beckoning me. Then he said to Madame, 'You see, he can't look us in the eye. His eyes are shifty like a pygmy's. He's dangerous. Natives are like that. When they can't look you in the eye it's a sure sign they've got some idea fixed in their wooden heads ...'

He grabbed me by the neck and forced me to look at him. I

did not resist. He turned his head and said to Madame:

'That's funny. You'd better get rid of him. I'll find you someone else. The place for this one is with me ... at *Bekön*,'* he added, using the word in my own language.

'Robert is attached to him,' said Madame, 'though I don't know what he sees in him ... I've asked him several times to sack him but you know how obstinate Robert is ...'

So, I was still at the Residence because of the Commandant. I was right to be frightened when he was away.

'It's no good pretending to be putting away the china,' said Madame, raising her voice. 'Open a bottle of Perrier and then leave us alone, Monsieur Toundi.'

I brought the bottle of fizzing water.

'Will Madame be wanting anything else?' I asked.

'No,' she said impatiently.

I bowed and backed out of the room. When I was beneath the veranda I heard the door shut and the key turn in the lock.

A song was running in my head. I noticed I was singing it out loud. It is a song we sing in French when someone is dying.

> *Shut the door, Saint Peter,*
> *Shut the door and hang up your keys*
> *He's not coming, he's not dying –*
> *Shut the door, Saint Peter,*
> *Shut the door and hang up your keys.*

* * *

Baklu with his right hand up to his nose was holding one of Madame's sanitary towels between the thumb and finger of his left. He tried to come into the kitchen. The cook shut the door against him and began to swear. Baklu went back to the wash-house, roaring with laughter. He came back a few moments

*Prison

later sniffing his fingers which were dripping with water and trying to dry them by waving them about in the air.

The cook half opened the door and shouted through, 'Don't come in here, don't come in here.'

'What's the matter?' said Baklu, laughing. 'You're getting very particular. Just to look turns you over. What about me, I have to wash it with my hands.'

He shook his hands about and went on:

'What do you expect. Everyone has his job. You're in the pots and pans and I'm in the washtub.'

The cook watched him, horrified. Baklu still went on.

'What amazes me is that you still haven't got over these things,' he said to the cook. 'It can't be the first time you've seen one of them ...'

The cook passed his hand over his face. 'It's not the same, seeing them,' he said, 'the eye seems to be a long way away. What would our ancestors say if they saw us washing things like that for the whites?'

'There are two worlds,' said Baklu, 'ours is a world of respect and mystery and magic. Their world brings everything into the daylight, even the things that weren't meant to be ... Well we must get used to it ... We laundrymen are like doctors, we touch the things that disgust ordinary men.'

'What are we to these whites?' asked the cook. 'Everyone I have ever worked for has handed over these things to the laundryman as if he wasn't a man at all ... these women have no shame ...'

'Shame, you talk about ...' burst out Baklu. 'They are corpses. Do corpses feel shame? How can you talk about shame for these white women who let themselves be kissed on the mouth in full daylight in front of everybody? Who spend all their time rubbing their heads against their husbands' cheeks or their lovers' more often, sighing, not caring where they are? Who are only good in bed and can't even wash their pants or their sanitary towels ... They say they work hard in their own country. But those who come here ...'

Baklu was going on with this when Madame appeared on the veranda. He looked at her, gave a little nod, and winked at us.

'Washman,' she called, 'what are you doing over there?'

'Nothing, Madame, I was just talking about my girl-friend...'

Madame bit her lip so as not to laugh. She forced herself to say, 'Back to work. This is not the time...'

Baklu hurried off towards the washhouse.

* * *

I was surprised today to see the doctor's wife appear on the steps outside the Residence. It was four o'clock and Madame was still not awake. I ran out to meet the doctor's wife and take her umbrella. She pushed me to one side, averting her head. She swept up the last two steps and on to the veranda. She hammered at the door. There was no answer. She turned around, came back to the top of the steps and hesitated. She realized reluctantly she would have to ask for my help. She raised her straggly eyebrows and spoke through clenched gold teeth.

I ran to Madame's bedroom. The door was open. She was asleep with her mouth open, one arm hanging down beside the bed, her legs crossed. There was a fly like a beauty spot on her cheek. She was wearing drawers and had undone her bodice revealing her firm breasts under the pink brassiere.

I coughed loudly and gave a little tap at the door. She sighed, opened her eyes and leapt out of bed, hastily covering her breasts.

I excused myself by saying, 'The doctor's wife is on the ver-anda.'

She buttoned up her bodice, watching me with a contained contemptuous anger.

'Show her to the living-room,' she said. 'You don't bother to knock on the door any more?'

'The door was open, Madame,' I said, 'but I knocked all the same.'

'That will do,' she said. 'Go and make up some lemon juice and Perrier water.'

She slammed the door on me. When I got back to the veranda the doctor's wife was powdering herself and pulling faces into a tiny mirror she held in the palm of her hand. She gave no sign that she had heard me come back. She was trying to stretch her non-existent lips as far as they would go. At each movement wrinkles sprouted as if by magic under her little lustreless eyes. She put away her mirror and compact. When she caught sight of me, she checked a nervous start. Again she raised her straggly eyebrows and stretched her mouth tight in a strange grin. I bowed and threw open the door of the drawing-room.

She stalked haughtily inside. I showed her a chair. At this point Madame appeared.

She had had time to slip on her grey silk dress and to compose her face. What a pleasure it was to receive a visit from the doctor's wife, she said, putting on a great air of delighted astonishment. The doctor's wife said how well Madame was looking and Madame pretended that she thought the tiny hat the doctor's wife was wearing was very smart. They talked about the heat and the next rains. The doctor's wife, like most old colonials, loved exaggerating. She asked after the Commandant, was full of his praise and then went on without a pause for breath to talk about Mme Salvain and her husband and then about all the other Europeans in Dangan. She mentioned a bout of malaria which had overtaken her husband and broke off only to give me a distant 'Thank you' as an indication that I should pour no more from the jug into her glass. Madame listened with now and then a little forced smile, holding her head between her thumb and finger. They raised their glasses, put them to their lips and then, almost in the same instant put them down again. The doctor's wife placed her hands together. She leant towards Madame and then flung herself against the back of her armchair with a little high-pitched laugh. Then she leant forward again. They smoked cigarettes. The doctor's wife began to repeat over again everything she had said since the conversation began. She talked of her daughter who was studying medicine in Paris, of next winter when she would see her again.

At first I listened to their conversation as I usually do, pretending to be busy in the room. When my ears were tired, I began to think of other things. I had lost all awareness of what they were saying, when a word from the doctor's wife roused my attention. I had just caught part of a phrase that she had spoken, leaning over, into Madame's ear.

'. . . it was yesterday, in the afternoon . . .' she was saying. They both looked at me at the same time and Madame went red. They took no more notice of me.

'You know,' said the doctor's wife, 'they think we can't understand their language. My boys jumped out of their skins yesterday when I caught them on the veranda pointing at M. Moreau who was passing your house. They were all talking and laughing and shouting, "Toundi, Toundi". I asked them what they were looking at and they told me that . . .'

The doctor's wife bent over farther towards Madame and they both turned and looked at me. Madame lowered her eyes.

'They are like that,' said the doctor's wife. 'Awkward and indiscreet. They are everywhere except where you want them . . .'

Though she was whispering right into Madame's ear I caught her last words.

'You ought to be careful . . . there is still time since your husband does not know . . .'

Madame was about to put her head into her hands but she checked herself, emptied her glass and wiped off the little drops of perspiration that studded her face The two women got up and went out on to the veranda. They talked together for a long time. The bugle from the police camp sounded half past five. Madame went with the doctor's wife as far as the road.

When she came back she called the cook to light the Aïda lamp. Lighting the lamp every evening at the hour when the first moths came brushing by was my job. Father Gilbert had taught me how to light a petrol lamp and I was rather proud of my special skill. At the Residence all the other servants were scared stiff to go near one of these lamps. There were several women in the location who had been widowed when a petrol lamp exploded in a houseboy's hands.

The cook pretended not to hear. Madame went to the kitchen. She went on pretending not to notice me, caught the cook's apron and indicated the lamp on the veranda. The cook waved his hands beseechingly and said that in all the years he had been working with Europeans he had never lit an Aïda lamp. Madame was not discouraged. She called for Baklu who at that time must have been somewhere in the location, sleeping off his beer.

Once more she pointed the cook to the veranda. He reared away like a sheep from the dip. Madame controlled a flash of anger and came towards me. She seemed to be making an effort to speak to me. I did not wait but went off to light the lamp.

The veranda, the courtyard and the kitchen were flooded with light. Madame was walking up and down. She crossed and recrossed the patch of shadow between the kitchen and the washhouse. The cook went across the yard with a steaming dish on his head.

I hurried to get the table laid. Madame came in. She did not raise her head or open her mouth through the meal. Afterwards, she said we could go.

*　　*　　*

Madame was writing letters. She raised her head from time to time and without seeing me her eyes wandered over the refrigerator I was polishing. She pushed away the table she had been writing on and went over to the bowl of flowers in the drawing-room. She picked a few petals of hibiscus and put them into an envelope. She moistened the flap with her little pink tongue and stuck it down. She got up, collected her papers and went into her bedroom.

'Boy, is my shower ready?' she called to me through the dividing wall.

'Yes, Madame,' I said.

She tried to whistle but soon ran out of breath and fell silent. The noise of a bottle smashing on the cement floor brought a sharp 'damn!' She called me to clear up the mess. It was one of the bottles of a preparation she puts on her face at night. Pieces of broken glass had gone under the bed. I knelt down and probing under the bed with the broom brought out not only broken glass but also some little rubber bags. There were two of them. Madame heard the sound of sweeping stop and looked round. When she saw me turning the little bags over and over with the end of the broom she sprang on me and tried to push them back under the bed with her foot. Instead she trod on one of them and a little liquid squirted out of it on to the floor.

'Get out,' she screamed. 'Get out. You don't know what they are?' she went on, out of control. 'You don't know? Contraceptives: contraceptives. Go on, tell everybody. What a subject for all the houseboys in Dangan to talk about. Go on. Get out.'

There are times when the anger of white people leaves you completely blank. While all this was going in I did not understand anything. Madame pushed me outside and I stood completely bewildered on the veranda.

The cook was watching from the kitchen window. He shook his head sadly, slapped his right hand against his left, and put the palm of his left hand up to his mouth. This was a way he had of indicating his astonishment. Today it merely irritated me. He turned his head and disappeared. I stood there, stunned, clutching my broom.

I went down the steps and into the kitchen. The cook had his back to me. For a good minute he did not speak. Then he said:

'Toundi, will you never learn what a houseboy's job is? One of these days you'll be the cause of real trouble. When will you grasp that for the whites, you are only alive to do their work and for no other reason. I am the cook. The white man does not see me except with his stomach. You lads of today, I don't know what's the matter with you. The white man hasn't changed since the Germans went. Only the language has changed. Ah, you lads of today, how you grieve us!'

He paused.

'What have you been doing to Madame this morning?'

He repeated his question.

'Don't look at me with those eyes,' he said, 'I am old enough to be your father. It is the voice of wisdom . . . outside his hole the mouse does not defy the cat.'

'What you say is true,' I said. 'But tell me . . . these little bags made of rubber . . . mustn't the houseboy . . .'

I was not allowed to finish. His face which a moment before had been so solemn was split from side to side by an enormous peal of laughter. He dropped down on to an empty packing case, shaken by spasms of laughter. He looked up at me and new gusts of laughter shook him. Baklu ran over from the washhouse.

'What's the matter?' he demanded, getting ready to laugh himself. 'What is it?'

The cook was holding his sides. He raised his arms towards me but another fit of laughter overtook him and he had to drop them. He pointed and wiped his eyes. Baklu bared his teeth. He was giving himself an advance on the laugh which the cook gasping, 'Wait, wai . . . wait' was promising him. After a while the cook grew calmer. He hitched up his trousers with his forearm. Then he went over to the sideboard. He was like a gorilla approaching a tree. He poured himself a little glass of wine, cleared his throat and came back to sit on the box.

'A chance to laugh like that,' he said, 'only comes once a year.'

He wiped his eyes again.

'Don't be so selfish,' said Baklu, impatiently. 'Are you putting a price on the news?'

'A wife!' said the cook bursting with laughter. He meant that this news was so expensive that he would have to tell him it for nothing.

'All right,' he began. 'Toundi and Madame have been quarrelling over little bags . . .'

'Little bags?' said Baklu, hanging his lip, pretending to be puzzled.

'The little rubber bags, you know . . . that the whites . . .'

He completed the sentence by grasping his private parts. Baklu folded in two and moved backwards step by step until his bottom bumped against the sideboard. He slid slowly to the ground and his shoulders rose and fell while he gave little dog-like yelps. The cook got up and went to thump him on the shoulder.

'It's a long time since I had a laugh like that,' said Baklu dusting the seat of his trousers.

'Come on, tell us about it!' the cook said, digging me in the ribs.

He did not give me a chance to begin before he burst out again, 'These whites with their craze for putting clothes on everything, even their . . .'

They both dissolved into laughter again.

'Still, what are they for?' said Baklu, putting on an act of innocence.

'To do things properly . . . They put it on, like a hat or a pair of gloves . . .' said the cook in an offhand, knowing manner, mocking my innocence.

'That's it,' said Baklu. 'It's the thing to wear for that particular occasion.'

They laughed again.

'Hey, I must go,' said Baklu, moving off; 'I've got a couple of baskets of dirty clothes . . .'

The cook sniffed and wiped his nose with the back of his hand.

'Never mind, lad,' he said to me. 'It's never out of season to have a good laugh even at a dead man's wake. You're not going to hold it against me for having a bloody good laugh, are you?'

He smiled and then became serious again.

'I suppose you've upset Madame,' he said. 'Your broom reached a bit too far. You see, it's a bit like you coming across M. Moreau's old man itself in the Residence. Women can't forgive a thing like that. It's worse than if you'd looked up her frock. A white woman just can't let her houseboy find things like that . . .'

He was trying hard not to laugh again. His strong lower jaw was shaking. He turned his back and I could see his neck quivering.

Madame appeared on the steps. She opened her mouth but no sound came from her throat. She called me at last and told me to bring my broom. She snatched it out of my hands and disappeared. A moment later I heard the faint scratching sound of straw on the cement.

'Looks as if she's going to sweep the bedroom herself,' said the cook. 'I only wish she'd try the cooking too.'

'She is sweeping her bedroom herself,' called Baklu in the vernacular. 'If only she would do her own washing!'

At eleven when Madame had finished dressing, the doctor's wife came to fetch her in the car.

'I shan't be in for lunch,' she told us. There was a slight quaver in her voice.

The car drove off. As soon as it was out of sight Baklu and the sentry joined us. They began to laugh again.

'I've heard all about it,' said the sentry. 'I thought I was going to split myself inside this belt.'

He plucked at his cartridge pouch.

'What are these Europeans going to think up next?' said the cook. 'They are already uncircumcized and yet they have to find other things to put round it.'

'The things they buy at the chemists stop their wives getting pregnant,' said Baklu. 'And they use them when they sleep with native women so that they won't get the disease. One of the orderlies told me . . .'

'If they don't want their wives pregnant why do they do it at all?' asked the sentry. 'They are mad, these whites. How can they say they are really doing it at all when it is just with a little bit of rubber?'

They discussed contraceptives all the afternoon.

Madame came back at four o'clock. She walked across the yard, her head bent. She vanished into her room and did not reappear until dinner. She hardly touched the chicken but ate a banana and drank her usual cup of coffee. She swallowed her tablets and told us not to go away before midnight.

When we left she was already snoring. The sentry helped me to shut the doors and windows of the Residence.

*   *   *

Madame asked the cook to find her a chambermaid and this morning he brought the girl he has found. He says she is the cousin of the niece of his sister's brother-in-law.

Very well developed at the back and her breasts still firm. She came barefoot, wearing a tailored jacket over her cloth and a single golden earring to set off her poverty. A real girl of the soil. Thick lips, black eyes and a sleepy expression on her face. She was waiting for Madame, sitting on the top step with a twig in her mouth.

The cook told us that he had only found out last night that they were related. Yes, she really was the cousin of the niece of his sister's brother-in-law.

'She's a town-girl,' he told us,' 'she's never been back to the village. The whites are all crazy about her behind, well you've seen it, those lovely elephant's livers bulging beneath her cloth . . . but she'll never make her fortune. Her parents must have eaten a travelling salesman. She can't stop still in one place. She lived on the coast with a white man. He was talking about marrying her and taking her home with him. And you know, when a white man marries a daughter of our people, she's usually something very special. The white man had no heart left, the cousin of the niece of my sister's brother-in-law swallowed it up in one night. They say you could see him sitting all day long with Kalisia – that's her name – on his bony knees. Then, one morning, Kalisia went off, just like that, when the birds were off at the end of the dry season. The white man cried and moved heaven and earth to find her again. They were frightened he would go out of his mind and the Commandant in charge there had him sent home. Kalisia had had enough of whites and she lived for a long time with one of the coast negroes you know, the ones with salty skins. Then she left him. She lived with other white men, other blacks, and other men who were not quite black and not quite white. Then she came back to Dangan like a bird comes to earth when it is tired of flying in the air . . .'

'And this is the one you have picked to be Madame's chambermaid?' asked Baklu, somewhat overwhelmed by this history. 'There are plenty of women down in the township . . .'

'Madame said I must find a clean girl who understood French and was not a thief. I couldn't have found anyone better. And what is more, she knows whites better than any of us,' he added, looking at each of us in turn.

'I'm afraid this girl will start trouble that will land us all in jail,' said Baklu. Any man with eyes can hardly see her without . . .'

The cook laughed.

'Are you talking about the Commandant or about one of us?' he asked. 'I know the Commandant. He's the kind of white man who will always suppress his feelings however strong they are . . . Besides, his wife is here; there is no danger. The Residence is not very big and I don't somehow see the Commandant climbing into a ditch . . .'

'You can't always rely on a sense of dignity in these matters,' said Baklu, 'especially with whites. Look at Madame . . .'

'We shall see,' said the cook. 'Women can sense these things. I can tell you that if Madame takes Kalisia on, it means that she doesn't think she's a danger . . .'

Nine o'clock came and Madame was still asleep. By now the heat of the sun had become overpowering. The skin began to toast pleasantly, Kalisia had stripped her shoulders. She drew her knees up under her chin and began to doze like the little grey lizard that was squatting in a scrap of newspaper just beside her. Baklu was stretched out on his stomach behind the washhouse and I was sitting at the top of the flight of steps waiting for Madame to wake up and letting a sense of warm well-being soak into my body.

Suddenly Madame's bedroom window opened. I woke up with a start. She rubbed her eyes and buttoned up the top of her pyjamas. She stretched herself, stifled a yawn and called me. She did not open the door but spoke to me through the partition. She sent me to change the water in her shower. She wanted to wash herself in cold water. At eleven o'clock, fresh as a day-old chick, she went on a tour of inspection of the rooms I had cleaned. She looked at the day's menu, went to see how much wine was left, drank the glass of lemon juice which I make for her every morning and began to go through the pile of letters waiting for her on the couch.

The cook came in. Madame asked him irritably what he wanted.

'Girl for chambermaid outside . . .' he said with a broad smile, bowing deeply.

The cook had a natural flair for showing respect. You have only to watch him making a bow before Madame or the Commandant. It begins with an imperceptible quivering of the shoulders. This gradually spreads through his whole body. Then his body as if it were under the sway of some mysterious force begins to bend slowly forward. He lets it go, his arms tight against his sides, his stomach pulled in until his head lolls on his breast. At the same time little dimples of laughter appear in his cheeks. When he has reached the position of a tree about to topple from the axe, he gives a broad grin.

Ever since Madame told him he was quite a gentleman the cook has felt his importance swelling daily after every bow.

He did not notice the icy look that Madame gave him over the top of the letter she was hurriedly reading.

'Where is she?' asked Madame.

The cook ran out and called Kalisia. She replied by a little humming sound and buttoned up her jacket. She pulled the twig she had been sucking out of her mouth and began to climb the steps nonchalantly. Everything about her seemed weary. She made no attempt to lift her feet which caught against every step as she climbed. She leaned in the doorway and gazed at us. Madame had gone back to reading her letter. She held it in one hand while with the other from time to time she tapped her cigarette-holder. The cook stood to attention by her side staring up at the ceiling.

At last Madame came to the end of her letter. She sighed and looked up at us each in turn.

'Bring the woman in,' she said to the cook.

He signalled to Kalisia. She coughed, passed her hand over her lips and stepped into the room.

Madame put her mail to one side and crossed her legs. Kalisia stared at Madame with that look of insolent indifference that always infuriates her when it comes from an African. The contrast between the two women was striking. The African was completely calm with a calmness that seemed nothing could ever trouble. She looked at Madame without concern, with the vacant look of a ruminant sheep ... Madame changed colour twice. Suddenly her dress became damp at the armpits. This wave of perspiration always heralded one of her rages. She looked Kalisia up and down. The corners of her mouth were turned down. She stood up. Kalisia was slightly taller. Madame began to walk round her. Kalisia although she pretended to be staring intently at her hands was now completely absent. Madame came back and sat down in front of her. She stamped her foot. The cook clicked his heels. Kalisia looked across to her kinsman, giving a tiny glance at Madame on the way. Madame went red. I turned my head away so as not to smile.

'Monsieur Toundi!' she thundered.

She lit a cigarette and inhaled. As she blew out the smoke her whole body seemed to go slack. Her forehead was beaded with drops of sweat.

'Have you been a chambermaid before?' she asked Kalisia.

'Yeeeeeesss,' said Kalisia with a smile.

'Where was that?'

'Over there – by the sea,' said Kalisia pointing with her arm westward towards the sea.

I could hardly hold myself. I bit my lips. Kalisia had a rather special idea of what her job was. I broke in and explained to Madame that she would have to put the question in a different way – something like, 'Have you ever been a lady's houseboy?' Kalisia gave an 'Ah' and told me in the vernacular that they would have had an interesting conversation at complete cross purposes.

Kalisia then admitted that she had never been a chambermaid in her life but that she would do her best to give satisfaction because from now on she did not want to earn her living in any other way. Madame seemed touched by this half-confession. At once, now that Kalisia had offered a kind of selfexcuse, Madame regained her air of superiority.

'I will see what I can do for you,' she said. 'Toundi will show you round.'

She dismissed us with the back of her hand.

'You can begin right away,' she called after us.

Kalisia followed me into Madame's bedroom.

'These whites are rich,' she said, looking round the room. 'I like working for whites like these. You know, when they are poor they are as mean as a catechist ... I once lived with a white man who used to count the lumps of sugar and measure the loaf after every meal. What are they like here?'

'All right when they are not angry,' I said. 'You'll see.'

'The mistress is beautiful,' said Kalisia. 'A white woman with eyes like hers can't do without a man. Let me see' (she went to peep at Madame through a crack in the door, 'I'd say she couldn't do without a man even for a fortnight . . . I bet she has a lover. Who is he?'

'You'll see for yourself,' I said.

'You rascal, you rogue, you sly devil,' she shouted. 'Slender hips like you've got are often the nest for a great big snake.' She pinched my buttocks. 'Don't think Madame doesn't know that as well!'

She made a grab at my sexual parts and gave a little hoarse cry.

'See, I was right,' she said. 'That's already had a taste of white flesh, I know. It's you. It's you that's Madame's man. I knew right away. You only have to look at her eyes when she talks to you.'

This was really too much. Her familiarity and abandon made me furious. I turned on her, my eyes blazing. She was dashed at once.

'I didn't mean to make you angry, my brother,' she said, so repentant that my anger quickly drained away.

'It doesn't matter,' I said. 'Only you went a little too far . . .' We both smiled. She winked at me and we turned Madame's mattress.

'What is she like?' she asked me after a pause.

'Who?' I asked.

'Madame,' she said.

I made a vague gesture.

'How many times do you do it a week?' she went on questioning.

I lifted up my arms in astonishment.

'Listen,' I said. 'Either you must keep your mouth shut or you must go back home. You may be crazy but I am not . . .'

'Oh, dear,' she said. 'So there really is nothing between you? Still, you're a man. Down on the coast, the houseboys sleep with their Madames, it's quite normal. Up here you're all too scared of the whites ... It's silly to be so scared, I can tell you ...'

'All right,' I cut her off.

We spread the coverlet over the bed. Madame came into the room and made no comment on our work.

'She really is a woman,' said the terrible Kalisia when Madame had gone.

Kalisia is going to work for two hours every day at the Residence. Still, she really is rather splendid.

* * *

The Commandant arrived out of the blue this afternoon. We were not expecting him before the end of the week. Madame herself seemed disconcerted.

The Commandant's face was drawn. In his crumpled grubby shorts he looked like a schoolboy who had been playing truant. He got out of the car without a word, picked up his briefcase, brushed his lips against Madame's forehead and made his way heavily to his room. Madame told us to unload the car and then went after him. She left the door open behind her.

She called to her husband and asked him what was wrong. He replied with a grunt. She went on badgering him and at last he said that she was looking too well to go worrying over him. She was silent for a moment. Then she told him he was being unfair.

She went and lay down in her hammock on the veranda and for a long time was lost in her thoughts. After he had rested the Commandant called for a shower. Later he appeared, shaved and pomaded. The colour had come back to his face. He had put on his white linen suit and was going through the official correspondence which the orderly had brought to Madame. She did not speak. The Commandant seemed to have forgotten she was there. He went into the garden and walked a little way from the Residence, his hands in his pockets. He came back towards the veranda and seemed to be going to his wife but he turned off into the drawing-room.

Madame got out of her hammock and in turn went into the garden. The Commandant called me and sent me to find her. She was staring straight in front of her, her chin between the thumb and finger of her right hand. She did not hear me coming and when I coughed she was startled. She listened to my message without a word and followed me back to the Residence.

When the Commandant called me I had the feeling he had just changed his mind about something and that was why he sent me to look for Madame. He was half lying down on the couch and holding something hidden in his hand. It was the time for the evening apéritif. When Madame came in I took up my position beside the refrigerator as an excuse to stay in the room. The Commandant did not look his wife in the eyes. He seemed distant and bitter.

'What is wrong with you?' his wife asked, touching his shoulder.

The Commandant shrank away. Then, noticing I was there, he allowed his wife to touch him. He kept his left hand clasped under the table. Madame's eyes and my own lighted on it at the same moment. He raised his glass with the other hand and emptied it at a single gulp. He called for some brandy.

'Brandy for Christ's sake,' he bellowed.

He filled up two glasses which he drank off one after the other. Madame tried to stop him. The Commandant pulled his arm away violently. Madame ran off into her room.

The Commandant tried to stand up but fell. He missed the couch and slipped down on to the floor. As I helped him up he swore at me. I had never seen him like this, even before Madame came. He managed eventually to get on to the seat again and stayed for a long time staring at the ceiling, his hands crossed on his stomach. Suddenly Madame burst out of her room and ordered me to go.

'No, let him stay,' shouted the Commandant, 'let him stay!'

He was sitting on the edge of the couch looking at his wife. She stood petrified in the middle of the room. Suddenly he hurled something at her. It slid along the floor towards the refrigerator. It was a lighter, M. Moreau's lighter. I had only seen it once, when M. Moreau came to dinner, but I recognized it.

Madame put her head into her hands and dropped into an armchair.

'What about that?' shouted the Commandant, pointing at the lighter. 'What do you have to say about that, eh, Madame Decazy?'

Sobs began to shake her shoulders but she controlled herself and raised her head arrogantly.

'Boy, leave us,' she said.

'Leave us?' shouted the Commandant. 'Are there any secrets between us? All the houseboys in Dangan know about it. Yes. You sleep with Moreau – the man you considered such a boor . . .'

Madame stood up. She walked up and down the room, wringing her hands. The Commandant watched her. His eyes were full of hatred. She walked up and down in front of him, glancing now and then at the lighter on the floor. Then she swung round and faced her husband. The Commandant's eyes passed over her shoulder and out through the open window beyond.

'We can't go on together after this,' said the Commandant. 'You didn't even give it a bit of time before you started deceiving me out here as well . . . and the natives had to know all about it before I did.'

He gave a pale smile and went on.

'For them I was "ngovina ya ngal a ves zut bisalak a be metua". Do you know what that means? Of course you don't. You never bothered to learn the local language. Well, it means everywhere I go I am now the Commandant whose wife opens her legs in ditches and in cars.'

'It's not true,' cried Madame. 'It's not true!'

She began to sob.

'And I did not know I had the honour to be cuckolded by Monsieur Moreau!' said the Commandant contemptuously, giving great stress to the word 'Monsieur'. 'This time you had to go down to the gutter to find yourself a lover.'

After a while he went on:

'If you knew how sickened I feel . . .'

Madame was crying. The Commandant lay down on the couch.

'Listen, my dear . . .' said Madame, lifting her face, the tears running down.

'I know, I know,' said the Commandant, smiling at the corners of his mouth. 'I know the old story. Your great weakness. How easily you go off the rails. The struggle between flesh and spirit. Well, I've had about enough of it, do you hear, I've had enough. You've always taken me for a fool. Ah, your outings in the car on Thursdays! That Monsieur Moreau you hardly ever mentioned and then only to despise him. You had them here to dinner because we must be careful not to look down on them just because they weren't quite our sort. My dear, I knew what you were up to . . . The natives were already calling me "Ngovina ya ngal a ves zut bisalak a be metua"! Only I didn't know it was with him . . . And you . . .' he shouted, lifting his head in my direction, 'you were the go-between, eh? For a cigarette from Moreau and a little present from Madame – eh?'

He shook his head sadly and dropped back on to the couch. Madame was still crying. The clock in the Residence chimed midnight.

The Commandant was watching me out of the corner of his eye and I could feel Madame's eyes through her fingers. I untied my apron. Before I went out on the veranda and hung it up as I did every evening after my work I bowed and wished them good night.

The Commandant stirred on the couch and turned against

the wall. Madame came and closed the door after me.

Outside the night was like pitch. A night without star or firefly . . .

*   *   *

Kalisia was listening open-mouthed. Every now and then she cracked her finger-joints with astonishment. When I had finished telling her what I had just seen she looked at me nervously and then turned away her head.

'If I were in your place,' she said, 'I'd go now before the river has swallowed me up altogether. Our ancestors used to say you must escape when the water is still only up to the knees. While you are still about the Commandant won't be able to forget. It's silly but that's how it is with these whites. For him, you'll be . . . I don't know what to call it . . . you'll be something like the eye of the witch that sees and knows . . . A thief or any one with a guilty conscience can never feel at ease in the presence of that eye . . .'

'But I'm not the only one who knows that Madame sleeps with M. Moreau . . .' I told her without much conviction. 'The Commandant himself said all the natives knew . . .'

Kalisia shrugged her shoulders and said:

'That doesn't make any difference . . . At the Residence you are something like . . . I don't know what to call it . . . something like the representative of the rest of us. I'm not talking about my kinsman the cook or Baklu – they are only men because they happen to have balls. . . . If I were silly enough to want to get married, I'd marry someone like you. I was saying though, that because you know all their business, while you are still here, they can never forget about it altogether. And they will never forgive you for that. How can they go on strutting about with a cigarette hanging out of their mouth in front of you – when you *know*. As far as they are concerned you are the one who has told everybody and they can't help feeling you are sitting in judgement on them. But that they can never accept

100

'... If I were in your shoes, I swear I'd go right away ... I wouldn't even wait for my month's wages.'

Kalisia looked at me as if she expected I would run off as she finished speaking. She clapped her hands, then she undid her cloth and retied it making a great knot under her jacket.

'All my blood has just trembled,' she said, 'as if I were going to hear bad news or something terrible were going to happen ... I always feel these things ...'

She would not look at me as we walked side by side towards the Residence. So that I would have to go on alone she went behind a bush and called:

'Go ahead by yourself. I am going to see Monsieur W.C. When you meet him you don't lift your hat, you lift your skirt.'

Her behind disappeared into a clump of grass.

Was I afraid? I don't think I was. Nothing that Kalisia had said to me seemed strange. There are things one prefers not to think about but that doesn't mean one forgets about them. When I left the Residence yesterday evening I looked round into the darkness several times. I thought I was being followed. I got home with a chilly sensation in my back. Lying on my mat I went over the scene at the Residence in my mind. There seemed no doubt that the Commandant was quite used to being deceived by his wife. I understand now why he pretended not to understand or not to hear when my country-men would greet him and shout after him 'Ngovina ya ngal a ves zut bisalak'. He would begin to whistle or else, to make it quite clear that he had not understood he would lean out of the car window with his finger raised against the brim of his topee.

*   *   *

Nothing today, except steadily mounting hostility from the Commandant. He is becoming completely wild. Kicks and insults have started again. He thinks this humiliates me and he can't find any other way. He forgets that it is all part of my job as a houseboy, a job which holds no more secrets for me. I wonder why he too refers to me as 'Monsieur Toundi' ...

* * *

I walked in on the Commandant and Madame kissing. I thought he would have held off longer. He was like a little boy caught stealing something he had pretended he did not want. Now I realize Madame can do whatever she likes.

'You ... Now you've started spying on us!' bawled the Commandant, panting for breath.

All through the evening he dared not look at me. Madame had a faint smile on her lips and her eyes were contracted to two round dots. She stared now at the Commandant, now at me and drummed on the table with her fingers.

* * *

The Commandant trod on my left hand. He was talking to Madame at the time and he went on talking as if he hadn't noticed. He managed to bring his foot down while I was off my guard, giving his boots a final polish before he went out. He has no memory and no imagination. He forgets he has already tried this on me and it did not make me cry out. As the first time he just walked on without looking round but this time he went jauntily like a man who feels pleased with himself.

* * *

The Commandant was sitting on the couch beside his wife with his head in a newspaper pretending to read. I finished clearing the table in the afternoon heat. The Commandant had not said a word. His looks are expressive enough, especially when he is angry. They had all been directed at me.

During the meal Madame made an unsuccessful attempt to question her husband on the kind of morning he had had. Then she fell into a daydream, only breaking off to serve herself as

102

the dishes came round. Now she was reading side by side with her husband. I could see his eyebrows moving over the top of his newspaper.

'It's hot,' he said, unbuttoning his khaki shirt. 'It's hot.'

'Why don't you take your shirt off and just sit in your vest?' said his wife.

He unbuttoned his shirt completely and pulled it out of his shorts but he did not take it off. His wife looked on, indifferent. She went back to her novel.

The Commandant called for a glass of water. When I brought it to him he asked if the water had been boiled.

'Yes, it is always boiled,' I said.

He picked up the glass of water between his thumb and finger and held it up to his eyes. Then he held it at arm's length, raised it above his head then brought it down again to eye-level. He brought it up to his nose, made a face, put it down on the tray and demanded another glass.

His wife almost imperceptibly shrugged her shoulders. I went back to the refrigerator and took the opportunity when the Commandant was not looking to spit – just a few tiny specks of spittle – into the clean glass I was filling. He drank it down and put the glass back on the tray without looking at me. He waved me away with a nervous movement of the back of his hand.

He folded up his newspaper, stretched himself and stood up. He began to sniff as if he had detected a bad smell. His nose turned first in one direction, then another, like a weather vane. It came to rest pointing towards one of the shutters which had been pushed to by the wind.

'There's a smell ... a smell in here. Open that shutter,' he ordered.

Madame twitched her nostrils and with a delicate movement of her body breathed the air all round her. She looked up at her husband whose back was towards her, and went on reading. When I had opened the shutter I came back, passing in front of the Commandant. He stopped me.

'Perhaps it's you,' he said, lifting up his nose, 'perhaps it's you.'

Madame looked up at the ceiling. The Commandant made a movement with his chin that I should stand farther away. He came back to the couch, tore off a strip of newspaper and went to wedge the shutter which I had just opened and which had not swung back.

'When there are natives about . . . everything must be kept wide open . . .' he said, trying to slip the paper into the hinge of the window.

He went out on to the veranda and lay down in an easy chair with his chest uncovered.

When I had finished I bowed to Madame and went off to the kitchen. As I walked across the veranda I heard the Commandant going back inside.

* * *

I was arrested this morning. I am writing this sitting on bruised buttocks in the house of the chief native constable who will hand me over to M. Moreau when he comes back off tour.

It happened when I was serving breakfast. The agricultural engineer and Gullet drew up outside with a screaming of brakes. They ran up the steps and apologized for disturbing the Commandant so early in the morning.

'It's about your houseboy,' said Gullet, twisting his neck in my direction.

The coffee-pot slipped from my hands and smashed on the cement floor.

'He knows why we've come,' said Gullet, warming to the business, 'don't you, my boy?'

The Commandant pushed away his cup, wiped his mouth and turned towards me. Madame smiled, curling up the left corner of her mouth. Sophie's lover seemed rather ill at ease. He asked Madame if he could smoke. It took him two attempts to get the cigarette alight. Gullet was completely composed.

'Now,' he began, 'M. Magnol's cook has disappeared with the workmen's wages.'

'This came to my notice at six o'clock,' said Sophie's lover with a quaver in his voice. 'The box had gone from my desk. I called my cook, whom you know,' he went on, nodding towards the Commandant. 'Her room was empty ... the bi ...'

He coughed so as he would not have to finish and to cover up that he had tried to correct himself when it was too late. Then he went red.

'She has gone off with my cashbox and my clothes,' he said, 'as well as her own things.'

He gave me a look as if he could slice off my head.

'It seems she is the fiancée-mistress of your houseboy,' said Gullet, rather proud of the compound noun he had invented. 'As soon as I was warned by M. Magnol I closed the frontier. My men are searching the location ... we thought your boy ...'

'How much was in the box?' asked the Commandant.

'A hundred and fifty thousand francs,' said the agricultural engineer, 'a hundred and fifty thousand francs.'

'I see,' said the Commandant, eyeing me.

His wife whispered something in his ear. I saw his eyes open wide. They talked together for a moment. The Commandant cleared his throat and pointed at me.

'Well, what have you got to say?'

. . . .

'Do you know the person involved?'

'Yes, Sir.'

'Where is she?'

. . . .

He put on his self-satisfied look, puffing out the underside of his chin and giving a list to his shoulders. Then, after a brief discussion with his wife, he rubbed his hands and without looking at me he said:

'Well, you will have to settle this affair with these gentlemen ...'

Gullet twisted his neck, Sophie's lover sighed. Madame called Kalisia.

'Give her your apron,' said the Commandant without looking at me.

'Come on, let's go,' said Gullet, getting to his feet.

The lover of Sophie went out first. They apologized once again to the Commandant and his wife. I went after the two white men. Big tears ran down Kalisia's cheeks as she tied my apron round her waist. It came right down to her ankles. Madame went over to her flower-bed, skipping like a little girl.

Baklu and the cook had not yet come to work. The sentry called down a vernacular curse on all white men.

Gullet and the lover of Sophie had come in a Land-Rover. So that I should not escape Gullet came in the back with me. The lover of Sophie drove. We took the road to the police station. Gullet held on to my belt and from time to time he trod on my big toe with his boots, all the time watching me closely. The agricultural engineer drove at speed, pedestrians scattered in panic as the Land-Rover lurched past.

'What's happened?' shouted my countrymen in our language, waving their hands.

Gullet drew me tighter and placed his hobnailed sole on my foot. In this way we drove through the Commercial Centre. Then we turned off to the police camp and stopped in front of a little discoloured tin shed. A tricolour fluttered over the roof. This was the police station. Gullet jumped down from the Land-Rover and dragged me with him. My knees were already bleeding. A constable ran up and then stood to attention. Gullet pushed me towards him. To show his enthusiasm for duty the constable struck me heavily on the neck with the edge of his hand. Everything was swallowed up in a great yellow flash.

When I came to I was lying face downwards on the ground. Gullet was astride my back, giving me artificial respiration. 'That's it,' said Sophie's lover, 'he's coming to . . .'

They got me to my feet. Gullet asked me where Sophie was.

'Perhaps she's gone to Spanish Guinea?' I said.

'How do you know?' shouted her lover.

'She told me ...'

'When, eh, when?'

'Eight months ago ...'

'You knew about last night?' said Gullet.

'No, Sir,' I answered.

'Then how do you know she was going to Spanish Guinea?'

'She told me she would eight months ago.'

'Anyway, you were her lover?'

M. Magnol's face darkened at that. He grabbed me by the neck of my jersey and stared into my eyes.

'Admit it,' he screamed, breathing foul breath into my face, 'admit it.'

I felt a terrible urge to laugh. The two white men watched in astonishment. Then Sophie's lover let me go.

Gullet shrugged.

'She's not my type,' I said, speaking to Gullet. 'She's not my type ... I used to listen to her talking to me without really seeing her ...'

Magnol's hands trembled. I thought he was going to fling himself at me. His face began to twitch all over. Little inarticulate noises came out of his mouth.

'It won't be easy with this one,' said Gullet. 'I don't think we'll get anything out of him. We'll go and search his place tonight ...'

They called the sergeant and whispered something in his ear. The constable handcuffed me and pushed me in front of him. We went into his house.

The sergeant is the head of the constables and his name is Mendim me Tit. It is the funniest name I have ever heard. The translation is 'meat-water'.

He's a kind of hippopotamus man. When he comes you

withdraw strategically unless you want to make a sudden appearance in front of Saint Peter's knocker.

When I was at the Residence I often used to say good morning to him and always fitted in a little conversation. He would listen to me with his huge arms behind his back and his protruding, strangely restless eyes seemed anxious to catch each word as it came out of my lips. Sometimes he laughed and that was really terrifying. The bray of an elephant and his face set in a fixed grimace which turned my bowels to water.

He was not one of our people. He had been brought here from somewhere over in Gabon. His arrival in Dangan had caused a sensation.

When we were inside the sergeant took off my handcuffs.

'We meet again, Toundi!' he said, patting me on the shoulder. 'You'll be all right here. But when you go to Moreau's . . .'

He trailed off into a vague gesture. The constable who had brought me clicked his heels and went away. Mendim me Tit patted me on the shoulder again.

'They haven't done much to you yet,' he said, taking a look at me. 'If they've sent you here though, that's what it's for . . . We must see what we can do. You must look bloody. We'll pour some ox blood over your shorts and jersey. Can you cry?'

We began to laugh.

'They think because I don't come from round here I'll have no mercy.'

We spent the day playing cards.

It was about eleven when Gullet and the lover of Sophie came to the police camp. I had splashed myself with ox blood and was lying down groaning . . .

Gullet shone his torch in my eyes and grabbed me by the hair. I don't know how I came to be really crying. I had been practising making little sobs and by the time they came I was crying as I had never cried in my life.

'Good,' said Gullet, letting go of my head. 'Now we can give his place a going over. Where is Sophie?' he asked me, grabbing me by the neck.

. . . .

'This is a tough one,' said Sophie's lover to egg him on.

'We shall see,' said Gullet giving me a kick in the kidneys.

They made me get into the back of the Land-Rover with Mendim. Gullet sat in front beside Sophie's lover. We drove off.

The headlights cut a bright path of light through the great drifts of darkness that had settled on sleeping Dangan. They picked out the last house in the European quarter. We climbed the next hill and then began to come down the other side towards the African township. It lay at the foot of the hill, built in what had once been a swamp. Soon it came into sight. Goats, drawn by the unusual brightness, came and gathered in the beam of our headlamps. Sophie's lover swung the wheel about nervously, to avoid them. Then he tired of this and bore down directly on the animals. The Land-Rover went skidding through the maze of decaying mud houses. I found it hard to pick out my own place among them.

'There, that's where I live, the house in the headlights now,' I said.

We pulled up. Gullet came over and spoke into my ear.

'Act as if you're just coming back from work in the ordinary way. Don't try any tricks or . . .'

He pushed me in front of him. I banged on the door. There was silence for a moment, then a familiar muttering.

'It's me, Toundi,' I shouted.

'Where have you been, this time of night?' the muttering said, coming closer.

'I've been at work,' I said.

'What's all that light? You haven't brought the sun home in your pocket by any chance?'

There was a sound of wood being moved and the door opened.

My brother-in-law brought his arm up in front of his eyes, blinded by the light. He adjusted his cloth.

'You should have told me you were ... But ... You're with Europeans ...'

He gave a broad smile and then bowed to Gullet and to Sophie's lover. He turned to me again and brought his hand up to his mouth when he saw the red stains on my jersey.

'What has happened, what has happened, my brother?' he cried in panic.

'Anyhow it's me, Joseph. You should have put the fire out. The house is full of smoke ...'

'There she is!' shouted Gullet grabbing me by the shoulder.

'It's my sister,' I said laughing. 'It's only my sister.'

'Make her come out into the light,' he called.

'Come and show yourself,' her husband told her.

My sister came out wrapped in a grubby sheet. Gullet turned towards the agricultural engineer.

'That's not her,' he said impatiently.

'Joseph, what have you done?' she asked me. 'Why are these whites with you?'

There were tears in her voice.

'What have you done, O my God,' she went on, 'what have you done ...'

'Nothing,' I said, 'nothing.'

She came forward and touched my jersey. Her scream shattered the silence of the night.

'What's going on? Who's dead?' someone called.

'The whites have come to arrest Joseph,' she wailed. 'They will kill him. His back is covered with blood.'

The whole location was strangely stirring. No one seemed left sleeping in the huts. A great circle had formed around us. Africans wrapped in blankets or cloths closed in. The worst thing to bear was the women. They gathered round my sister, wailing shrilly and tearing their hair. My sister kept shouting that the whites were going to kill her brother, the only brother she had in the world.

110

I felt embarrassed. This custom of useless lamentation over other people's misfortunes irritated me.

Gullet called for silence. He walked into the crowd brandishing his whip. He cleared a space in front of him. He said something quietly to Sophie's lover. He signalled the constable to grab my shoulder and hold me so that I could not go with the Europeans into the house.

'Everyone stay outside,' said Gullet. 'We are going to search.'

'There go all my water jugs again,' moaned my sister, 'all my poor jugs.'

She tried to follow the Europeans into the house but the constable pushed her back.

'Don't let him eat my bananas,' she persisted. 'Don't let Gullet eat my bananas.'

Laughter spread among the crowd. The constable put his large hand up to his mouth to hide his own laughter.

The Europeans were busy in the house. Everything that could be moved they kicked into the yard. It sounded like a storm raging inside the house. They turned out a mattress made of dead banana leaves sewn up in an old sack. Gullet took out his knife, slit it open and began to examine the filling, leaf by leaf. The constable and Sophie's lover helped him. They soon gave up. Sophie's lover was the first to straighten himself. He wiped his fingers with his handkerchief. Gullet called my brother-in-law.

'Do you understand French?' he asked him.

My brother-in-law said he didn't, shaking his head from side to side. Gullet twisted his neck towards the constable who clicked his heels and took up position in between the white man and my brother-in-law.

'Ask him if he knows Sophie,' said Gullet to the constable.

The constable turned to my brother-in-law.

'The white man asks if you know whether the woman we are looking for is Toundi's girl-friend,' he said in the vernacular.

My brother-in-law raised his right arm. He bent his index

finger and folded his thumb over it. The other three fingers remained straight. This meant that he swore before the Holy Trinity the truth of what he was going to say. He moistened his lips with his tongue and then in a deep, harsh voice he said that there had never been anything between Sophie and myself and if he lied might God strike him down on the spot.

'Let him slay me,' he shouted.

The constable translated that my brother-in-law was a good Christian. The two Europeans looked at him in some astonishment but he went on, unperturbed.

'He is a good Christian who will not swear lightly. He swears it is the truth that he knows nothing.'

'And his wife?' said Gullet, pointing to my sister.

She raised her right hand as well. The lover of Sophie stopped her before she went further.

'Right, that's enough of that!' he shouted. 'No one knows Sophie – not even you, eh?' he added looking at me.

'Tell them that anyone who tells us where Sophie is hiding will get a present,' said Gullet to the constable as we came out of the house.

The constable clapped his hands and spoke to the crowd that was melting away into the night.

'If you want to have plenty of money,' he said, 'inform against Sophie . . . you might even get a medal . . .'

'What do these uncircumcized think we are?' someone shouted.

'Right,' said Gullet, turning to me. 'We're going to put you in a safe place while we continue our inquiries. Let's go.'

To show his thoroughness Mendim pushed me roughly towards the Land-Rover. An indignant murmur came from the crowd.

Gullet sat down next to the lover of Sophie who was banging on the steering wheel with his fists and muttering 'The bitch . . . the bitch . . .' He backed and then flung round the wheel. The crowd scattered in panic.

'Give him twenty-five blows of the sjambok,' Gullet told the constable when we got back to the police camp.

I lay down on my stomach in front of the constable. Gullet handed him the hippopotamus-hide whip he always carried. The constable made it hiss down on to my buttocks twenty-five times. When it started I determined not to cry out. I must not cry out. I clenched my teeth and forced myself to think of something else. The image of Kalisia came up before my eyes. It was followed by Madame's image and then my father's . . . the day's events passed before my eyes.

Behind my back Mendim was beginning to pant.

'Scream, for God's sake,' he yelled in the vernacular, 'cry out. They'll never let me stop while you won't cry . . .'

He counted twenty-five, then he turned round to the whites.

'Give me the whip,' said Gullet.

He brought down the hippopotamus-hide lash across the constable's back. The constable gave a roar of pain.

'See, that's how I want him whipped. Start over again!'

Mendim rolled up the sleeves of his khaki jacket, his lips twisted in pain.

'Scream, scream,' he begged as he went to work on me again. 'Are your ears blocked with shit?'

The lover of Sophie shouted at him to shut up. He gave me a kick under the chin. Then he called 'Stop, stop.'

Mendim stopped.

'Tomorrow, nothing to eat . . . Understand?' said Gullet turning me over with his foot. 'You will bring him to my office in the afternoon. All day, the whip . . . Understand?'

'Yes, Sir,' said Mendim.

The whites went off.

I could hardly have expected to spend the night in Mendim me Tit's house. He is dozing in front of me, his mouth open, huddled in an old armchair like an old overcoat.

'I think I've done something today that I shall never be able to forget or to make up for ...' he said to me when the whites had gone.

His great eyes grew dim with tears.

'Poor Toundi ... and all of us,' he moaned.

SECOND NIGHT AT THE
POLICE CAMP

There are about twenty of us 'in trouble' who take the water round to all the white houses in Dangan. This is the water-party. The well is down at the bottom of the hill more than a kilometre from the European quarter on the slopes above it.

My can had a hole in it. I stopped it up as best I could with clay but the water still ran down on to my shoulders. The worst was climbing up the hill with a can of water on my head and a constable behind me with a whip. We ran back downhill to the well and then all over again ... By midday I thought my head would crumple up. It's lucky I've got tough wiry hair so that my can could rest on it like a cushion.

I felt pleased to think that neither the Commandant nor M. Moreau nor Sophie's lover ... nor any other European in Dangan could have stood up to it like we did.

At midday, a visit from Kalisia.
Tears to laughter and back again. A packet of cigarettes.
News from the Residence.
I am not mentioned any more. Perfect love between Madame and the Commandant – or so they pretend.

At one o'clock, a visit from Baklu.
His lips trembled. A little money.
News from the Residence.
I am completely forgotten. Madame loves her husband, but sometimes looks out of the window to watch the cars passing. Is she hoping to see M. Moreau come back? He would have to pass the Residence. There is no other way to his house.

Visit from my sister.

Much crying. You would think she had lost her husband. She has not washed since I was arrested. Lines of tears and snot on her face. What a way of expressing sorrow, to make yourself disgusting. But it is the custom. As long as I am here she will go on crying until she has driven her husband mad and the poor man is too afraid to ask her for his food.

She brought me a little money, just enough to put into Mendim's big hand. He is my guardian angel. She told me not to get excited as if this would help in not provoking the whites.

Poor sister. She is quite the little mother now with her advice, her worried frown, her eyes dimmed with tears. Yet how moved I was . . .

Visit from my brother-in-law.

We have our own way of talking. We ask questions and the only answers are other questions. There was a moment of emotion when we met again with the guard looking on. My brother-in-law broke the silence with, 'Where is it all leading to?' and 'What kind of people are we . . .?' and waving his arms.

There was nothing for me to say except just as he was leaving to ask him the same question.

Visit from Obebe the catechist.

A tedious little old man. It was as much as I could do to control myself throughout his visit. Talked at length about the Passion of Our Lord. Perhaps he thinks I'm a new Christ. He recommends forgiveness and speaks of the rewards and blessings of the Lord and tells me about heaven as if my arrival there was only a matter of days. He still suffers from the gonorrhoea he has had since before the war. His spiritual concerns did not keep him from taking a share of our tiny meal. He promised to come again tomorrow.

Mendim is going to get rid of him for me.

*   *   *

Water-party.
Water, sweat. Whip, blood.
Up the slope, killing. All in.
I cried.

*   *   *

I vomited blood. My body has let me down. There is a shooting pain through my chest like a hook caught in my lungs.

This morning Mendim took me to Gullet. At first he wouldn't listen.

'You can't put it over on me as easily as that,' he said, stiffening his neck. 'Not quite as easily as that.'

He got up from his desk and came over. He turned my head in various directions. He put a damp hand on my forehead and pulled a face. Then he took my pulse.

'Right,' he said and went back to his chair.

He took out a book and asked me my name. When he had finished writing he gave the book to Mendim who clicked his heels.

'Take him to the doctor,' he said. 'We'd better clear this up ... As for you,' he said, looking straight into my eyes, 'don't think this means I won't be questioning you again this afternoon.'

We went out.

All I knew about the hospital were the discoloured walls that had once been yellow I glimpsed over the top of the hibiscus hedge as I went to market. There are two places that terrify the natives in Dangan. One is the prison and the other is the hospital. Everyone calls it 'The Blackmen's Grave'.

At last we got there.

Dangan Hospital is between the Administrative Centre and the Commercial Centre. There are about a dozen small identical buildings arranged around a central lawn. In the middle of the lawn is the red and yellow Operating Theatre.

An African orderly saw us and came up to Mendim with his arm outstretched and a broad grin on his face. I realized from his jauntiness he must be afraid. He was afraid of Mendim like all the others we had passed, feverishly removing their hats as we went by. Without any sign from Mendim he offered him a cigarette and was upset to find he did not smoke. He felt in his pockets and brought out a kola nut. He broke the nut in two and offered one piece to Mendim. He tossed the other into his own mouth. The orderly then pulled a face.

'What's wrong with this fellow?' he said. 'Is he malingering?'

Mendim drew his head into his shoulders and stopped chewing. He spat between the orderly's legs.

'Oh, I'm sorry,' said the orderly, 'we often get malingerers among your prisoners.'

Mendim spat again, on to his shoes. The orderly stood aside.

'I'm so-o-o sorry,' he stammered behind us.

'They're all like that,' said Mendim, 'all the same . . . he knows sooner or later I'll run across him again . . . so he goes on like that . . .'

We went towards the dispensary. The patients were waiting two deep outside a door marked 'Doctor's Surgery'. The queue was really too long for the veranda and the constable on duty had somehow to keep all the people waiting inside the tiny space. All the illnesses in the world touched and jostled, sweated and squeezed, surging backwards and forwards every time the door opened or shut. There were terrible cases of yaws, all pocked like cassava stalks, there were lepers with cracked and blistered skins, sufferers, from sleeping sickness with their far-away look, pregnant women, old women, whimpering babies . . .

As soon as he saw Mendim the constable stood to attention. Mendim gave the order, 'At ease'. With his baton he cleared a path for us both through the crowd of patients. He knocked on the door of the surgery. Another constable was behind the door. He opened it a little but when he saw Mendim, he came out and respectfully, he ushered us inside.

'There's no one here yet,' he said, 'it's only ten o'clock. The African doctor is doing an operation at the moment. As soon as he has finished consultations will begin. The white doctor is never here. He's just been made a captain . . .'

I sat down on the bench. I was thirsty. I felt a needle pass through my lungs from one side to the other. I couldn't breathe deeply because of the weight on my ribs. Mendim was sitting opposite to me. He kept turning the pages of the medical examination book and nodding his head.

'Why didn't you tell me you got a rifle butt in your chest yesterday?' he asked suddenly.

. . . . .

'A butt in the chest from Djafarro is not a thing you get over,' he went on. 'I must say it puzzles me – your countrymen in the north are real savages . . .'

There was a great stir beyond the door. The African doctor came in. He shook hands with us, hung up his topee and sat down at his desk.

He was a man who must have been nearing forty but his slimness made him look younger. The tattoo marks between his eyebrows were made a few years after the first war.

He told me to undress. He moved his stethoscope over my back, then put it on my chest and told me to breathe in. He frowned and for a fraction of a second a look of horror crossed his face. Then he became impassive again. He took the stethoscope from his ears, lit a cigarette, got up from his chair and sat down on the table in his office.

'Another rifle butt . . .' he began. 'I'll have to X-ray. Trouble is I haven't got the keys of the X-ray room. The doctor in charge isn't here . . .'

He got up and stubbed his cigarette fiercely into the ashtray.

'He's not here . . . he's never here,' he said as if to himself.

He came over and put his hand on my shoulder.

'I'm going to send you to hospital ... Don't be afraid, everything will be all right. I'm going to make a report to the Chief of Police.'

He wrote for ten minutes and gave the letter to Mendim. He clicked his heels and left. The doctor called an orderly.

Another orderly rushed into the office with a bottle under his arm. 'He's not there,' he said.

He banged the bottle on the table. 'Some more arcoo,' he said, 'some more arcoo.'

He pulled off his cap and mopped his forehead. He was a huge frog-like man with a squashed face, as if it had been punched in. His coat and overalls were unbuttoned to give room for his great belly. A little gold chain disappeared into one of the folds of his great bull-neck and reappeared on his Adam's apple where a tiny metal Christ hung suffering, bathed in the gross black man's sweat.

The doctor glanced at him indifferently and showed him the door. The orderly hesitated, picked up the bottle and staggered towards the door.

'O.K., O.K.,' he said laughing. 'O.K., Chief.'

The stench of alcohol and ether that had filled the office vanished with him.

I felt cold. Even in the strong sun, my teeth chattered. A numb weariness filled me. I felt light, a thousand pairs of bellows quickening my breathing. My thoughts came to a stop. The doctor's white coat rose up, covered me, covered the whole room. It was floating down there over Father Gilbert's grave, over his motor cycle, over the 'Hammer of the Whites'. I was at the top of the cotton tree high up among the branches. The whole world stretched out at my feet, a great sea of people with leprosy and yaws, pregnant women with their bellies slit open and slimy old men, and millions of Gullets perched on the anthills kept order, cracking their hippopotamus-hide whips ... I took off from my branch and dived headfirst plunging a thousand miles down on to that world. My head burst like a bomb. Now I was only a cloud, a cloud of fireflies, a bright dust of fireflies swept on the wind . . . then blackness . . .

When I came to I was lying on a mat in a wooden bed, alone in a small cubicle. The partitions came down nearly to the floor. From my bed I could see only people's feet. The handle on the door of my cubicle turned. I shut my eyes.

'He's not awake yet,' said a voice I recognized as the African doctor's.

He took my wrist and laid his hand on my forehead. Then he went away. The handle of the door turned again. I heard the noise of bare feet on the ground. An ordinary African, like me. I opened my eyes and saw a scarred face under a red chéchia. He was standing to attention. It was a Sara. I made signs that I was thirsty. He threatened me with his bayonet. I lay still. I had a terrible headache.

At six o'clock the African doctor came back. This time the white doctor and Gullet were with him. They pulled back the blankets while the African doctor explained. He said that I must have a broken rib which had perforated my bronchia.

'We'll see about that tomorrow,' said the white doctor. 'Meanwhile, what about his temperature . . .?'

He looked at my chart.

'. . . only 103 – that's not serious for them. He won't slip through your fingers,' he said, to reassure Gullet.

They made me swallow some pills. The African doctor pulled the blankets back over me. They went away.

At midnight I was pretending to be asleep. The Europeans came back by themselves. The doctor told the others what the African doctor had told him. I opened my eyes just enough to see. M. Moreau was there. He was swaying backwards and forwards on his feet. How happy he looked!

'He must have his punishment,' he said. 'Take care of him and send him to me. He's a dangerous element. I shall make him talk . . . I shall set to work on him tomorrow.'

The Europeans went away.

The orderly came to see me on his round. He wore his white

coat directly over his underpants. He looked at me hard and took my hand.

'No,' he said, 'I don't think you did what they say. I always know. You're not capable of a thing like that. There's something else behind it all. I wonder why you are such an important patient. When the whites have decided to get one of us they always get him ... I wonder why you don't get out. No one will believe you while there's only you to tell the truth ... You're only good for Spanish Guinea ... or the prison cemetery ...'

I must get away ... Go to Spanish Guinea. M. Moreau is not going to have me ...

The constable is snoring already. The hospital clock has struck three in the morning.

I must take my chance. But it's a slim one ...

Miguel de Cervantes Saavedra (1547-1616) es el escritor más importante de la literatura española. Es, además, el autor español más conocido fuera de España.

En tiempos de Cervantes, España es un país cada vez más pobre y menos fuerte. Y el escritor vive la historia española en su propia carne: toma parte en las guerras contra los turcos y pierde una mano en la batalla de Lepanto. Pasa cinco años en Argel como prisionero de guerra. Ya de vuelta a España, sólo consigue trabajos que apenas le dan dinero. En 1597 va de nuevo a la cárcel por problemas de dinero y de trabajo...

Además de El ingenioso hidalgo don Quijote de la Mancha, *Cervantes escribe, entre otras obras, las* Novelas ejemplares. *Éstas se abren con sus famosas palabras: «Yo soy el primero que ha escrito novelas en lengua española».*

Las Novelas ejemplares *son doce novelas cortas donde Cervantes recoge ideas y asuntos muy diferentes. Pero lo hace siempre desde un juego literario que presenta, a un mismo tiempo, la cara alegre y la cara triste de la vida.*

Así ocurre en Rinconete y Cortadillo, *la historia, llena de humor, de una cofradía de ladrones.*

EL ESPAÑOL DE CERVANTES

Las formas de tratamiento en el español de los siglos XVI y XVII eran distintas a las actuales:

1. En lugar de «usted», para el trato cortés se usaba **vuestra merced** (plural: **vuestras mercedes**) con el verbo en tercera persona:
   Ej.: «¿De dónde es vuestra merced y adónde va?»
   (en vez de «¿De dónde es usted y adónde va?»).
   Ej.: «Vuestras mercedes sólo tienen que llevar la carne, la fruta o el pescado al sitio que manda el cliente.»
   (en vez de «Ustedes sólo tienen que llevar...»).
   De **vuestra merced** tratan todos a Monipodio. Así se tratan también Rinconete y Cortadillo cuando se ven por primera vez.

2. En lugar de «tú», para el trato entre iguales o para dirigirse a un inferior se usaba **vos** con el verbo en segunda persona del plural. **Vos** tiene siempre un matiz de cortesía:
   Ej.: «¡Eh, chico! ¡Vamos! ¡Tenéis que ayudarme!»
   (en vez de «... ¡Tienes que ayudarme!»).
   Ej.: «Pues yo os voy a llamar a vos, Rincón, Rinconete, y a vos, Cortado, Cortadillo.»
   (en vez de «Pues yo os voy a llamar a ti, Rincón, Rinconete, y a ti, Cortado, Cortadillo.»).

En plural se usaba **vosotros** con el verbo en segunda persona de plural.

De **vos** se tratan Rinconete y Cortadillo entre sí, una vez que son amigos. De **vos** también trata Monipodio a sus hombres.

3. **Tú** se utilizaba solamente en el trato muy familiar o con gente muy inferior:

Ej.: «Vamos a ver, después de pegarte no te dio un beso el Repolido.»

De **tú** se tratan las prostitutas entre sí y de **tú** tratan a sus hombres. De **tú** trata también Monipodio a estas chicas.

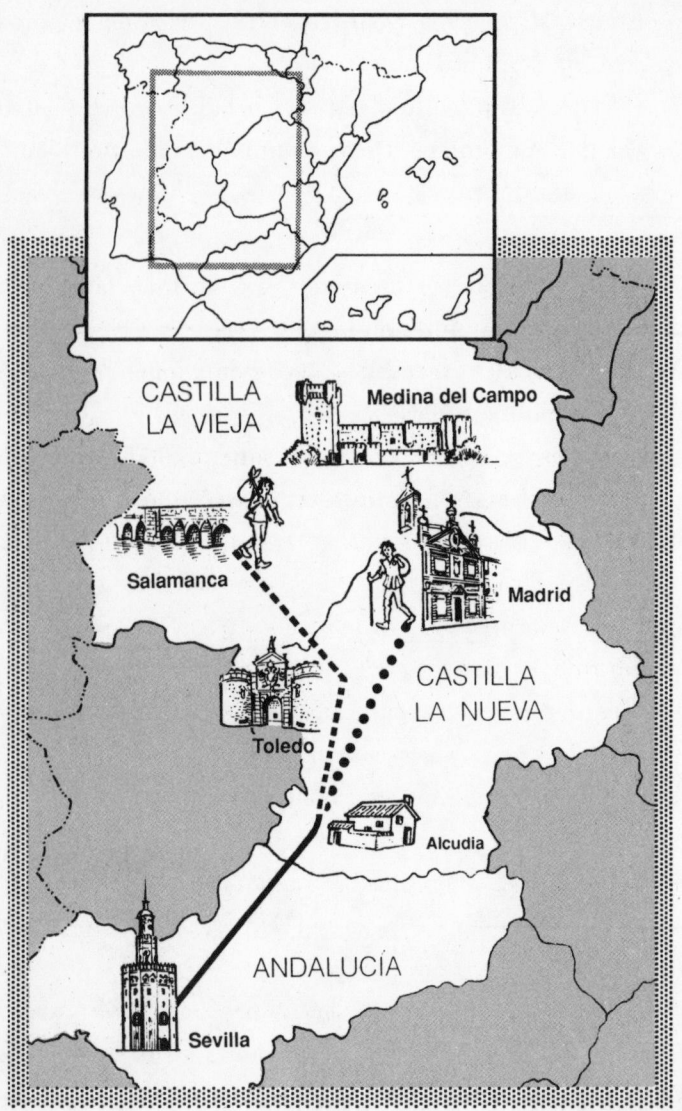

I

Eɴ los campos de Alcudia, entre Castilla y Andalucía, está la venta[1] del Molinillo. Un día de verano de mucho calor llegan allí, por casualidad, dos chicos de catorce o quince años de edad. Los chicos son guapos, pero están negros por el sol que han tomado en los caminos. Sus manos no están muy limpias, sus pantalones son muy viejos y sus zapatos están rotos. Ninguno de los dos tiene capa[2], pero usan sombrero y llevan armas: uno su espada[3] medio rota; el otro un cuchillo de cocina.

Los dos chicos descansan en el portal que está delante de la venta. No se conocen, pero sentados allí, uno al lado del otro, empiezan a charlar:

–¿De dónde es *vuestra merced*, señor, y adónde va? –pregunta el chico que parece mayor.

–No sé de dónde soy, caballero[4], y tampoco sé hacia dónde voy –contesta el más joven.

–¿Tiene *vuestra merced* alguna profesión?

–Sí, claro. Yo sé cortar[5] pantalones y chaquetas. Mi padre, que es sastre[6], me enseñó, y la verdad es que lo hago muy bien... Pero tengo mala suerte y no consigo encontrar trabajo.

–Eso le ocurre siempre a la gente buena. Pero *vuestra merced* es todavía joven y puede cambiar su vida. Seguro que sabe hacer otras cosas y no me las ha dicho, ¿me entiende? –pregunta sonriendo el chico mayor.

–¡Hombre!, es que hay cosas que no debemos contar a todo el mundo –contesta el otro.

–Señor, yo también sé tener la boca cerrada, pero ahora me voy a presentar a *vuestra merced*. Y es que pienso que la suerte nos ha traído hasta aquí para hacernos amigos. Yo me llamo Pedro del Rincón. Mi padre es un hombre importante, que vende bulas[7] para la Santa Iglesia. Yo le ayudaba en su trabajo, pero pronto me di cuenta de que me gustaban más los reales[8] que las bulas. Pues bien, un día cogí todo el dinero que pude y me fui a Madrid. Allí, en pocas semanas, me lo gasté todo. Pero vinieron a buscarme los guardias por haber robado dinero de la Iglesia y tuve que salir de la ciudad... Y aquí estoy, caballero. Gracias a Dios, tengo estas cartas[9] y con ellas consigo bastante dinero para vivir.

En ese momento Rincón saca unas cartas sucias y rotas que guarda debajo de su camisa.

–La verdad es que juego muy bien a la veintiuna[10]. Pronto lo va a ver *vuestra merced*.

En este momento Rincón saca unas cartas sucias y rotas que guarda debajo de su camisa.

–Bien, señor. Ahora le voy a contar yo mi vida. Me llamo Diego Cortado y soy de un pueblo que está entre Salamanca y Medina del Campo. Como le dije, mi padre es sastre y me enseñó su profesión. Pero no me divertían los pantalones y chaquetas y empecé a cortar otras cosas. Y es que ¡me gustan tanto las bolsas[11]!, sobre todo si están llenas de dinero... La vida en el pueblo era bastante aburrida y decidí irme a Toledo. Allí, en sólo cuatro meses, hice unos trabajos maravillosos: robaba a las mujeres en el mercado y no se daban cuenta; cortaba todas las bolsas que encontraba... ¡De verdad que soy un buen sastre! Pero, un día, alguien le contó mis aventuras al Corregidor[12] y este caballero me llamó para conocerme. Yo preferí no visitar a un señor tan importante y me fui de la ciudad.

–Bueno –dice Rincón–, ahora ya nos conocemos mejor. No tenemos ni dinero, ni zapatos ni caballos, pero creo que vamos a entendernos.

–Yo también lo creo –contesta Cortado.

Los chicos se dan la mano como amigos. Rincón saca otra vez las cartas de debajo de su blusa y le explica varios trucos[13] a Cortado. Después los dos empiezan a jugar a la veintiuna.

II

A los pocos minutos, sale un viajero al portal y se sienta a jugar con ellos. Rincón y Cortado le hacen sus trampas[14] y en un momento le ganan diez reales. El viajero, enfadado, intenta coger su dinero, pero uno saca su espada y el otro su cuchillo y empiezan a pelear[15]. Por suerte para los jóvenes, en ese momento pasan por delante de la venta varios hombres a caballo. Cuando ven a un hombre tan grande pelear con dos chicos tan pequeños, bajan de sus caballos para ayudarlos. En seguida ponen fin a la pelea.

Los hombres van hacia Sevilla y proponen a los chicos viajar con ellos.

—Con *vuestras mercedes* vamos —dice Rincón.

Y, sin más palabras, el joven se sube a un caballo. Cortado hace lo mismo y allí se queda el viajero, solo y más que enfadado, pero sin poder hacer nada.

Durante el viaje a Sevilla, Rincón y Cortado tienen ocasión de abrir las maletas que llevan sus nuevos señores, pero no lo hacen. No quieren tener más problemas.

Sólo cuando ya están llegando a la ciudad, en un momento en que nadie lo mira, Cortado abre uno de los bolsos y saca de él dos camisas, un reloj de sol y alguna cosa más.

Ya en Sevilla, Cortado y Rincón dicen adiós a los caballeros y corren hacia el mercado del Arenal. Allí venden las dos camisas por veinte reales. Después, se van a ver la ciudad. Visitan la Iglesia Mayor y al final de la mañana llegan cerca del río. En la plaza, ven a muchos jóvenes correr de un lado a otro con una cesta[16] en la mano.

–¿Qué hace *vuestra merced*? –pregunta Rincón a uno de ellos–. ¿Cómo es ese trabajo en que está tan ocupado?

–¿Podría *vuestra merced* contarnos qué dinero saca al día y si el trabajo es cansado? Somos nuevos en Sevilla y no tenemos nada en que ocuparnos.

–Es un trabajo tranquilo. *Vuestras mercedes* sólo tienen que llevar la carne, el pescado o la fruta al sitio que manda el cliente. En un día pueden ganar bastante dinero. Además, siempre pueden coger alguna cosa de la cesta. Pero el cliente no debe darse cuenta, ¿eh...?

A Rincón y a Cortado les parece bien el trabajo y con el dinero de las camisas, compran tres cestas: una para la carne, otra para el pescado y otra para la fruta. El joven de la plaza les explica dónde pueden trabajar:

–Por las mañanas hay que ir a la plaza de San Salvador, los días de pescado a la Costanilla, y todas las tardes al río.

III

A la mañana siguiente, Cortado y Rincón llegan temprano a la plaza de San Salvador. Allí los esperan sus primeros clientes: un estudiante y un caballero. El estudiante habla con Cortado; el caballero llama a Rincón:

–¡Eh, chico! ¡Vamos! Tenéis que ayudarme.

–Encantado, señor. Hoy es mi primer día de trabajo y *vuestra merced* es mi primer cliente.

–Pues tenéis muy buena suerte, porque pienso pagaros bien por el trabajo. Hoy invito a comer a unas amigas de mi novia y quiero llevar estos paquetes a su casa.

–Muy bien, señor. Yo soy fuerte y puedo llevar los paquetes más pesados. Además, si es necesario, puedo también preparar la comida a las señoras...

El caballero se ríe, y empieza a meter cosas en la cesta de Rincón, hasta dejarla llena del todo. Luego le dice dónde está la casa de su novia y le paga. Rincón se va con los paquetes y a los pocos minutos está de vuelta en la plaza. Allí lo espera Cortado, que saca de su blusa una bolsa de color amarillo, llena de escudos[17] de oro.

–El estudiante me ha pagado con esta bolsa, además de darme dos escudos. Pero creo yo que debéis guardarla *vos*. Así yo me quedo más tranquilo.

Rincón coge la bolsa y la mete con cuidado entre su ropa.

A los pocos minutos vuelve a la plaza el estudiante, muy nervioso y con el color de la cara cambiado.

–¿Habéis visto la bolsa que llevaba yo hace un momento? –le pregunta a Cortado.

–No, señor, lo siento –contesta éste muy tranquilo–. Yo no la he visto.

–¡Ay! ¡Pobre de mí! –grita el estudiante–. Seguro que la he dejado en algún sitio y alguien me la ha robado.

–¿Robar a *vuestra merced*? –pregunta Cortado–. No lo creo. *Vuestra merced* es persona que trabaja para la Iglesia, ¿no es verdad?

–Pues sí –contesta el estudiante–. Yo recojo el dinero de la Iglesia, ¡y ése es el dinero que me han robado!

–¡Oh! Entonces el asunto es muy serio –dice Cortado–. ¡Pobre del ladrón! No me cambio por él. Pero yo, señor, le voy a dar un consejo. Debe estar tranquilo. Todo tiene solución en esta vida. Porque de la nada nos hizo Dios y detrás de un día viene otro día y...

–¡Callaos ya, chico. Por vuestra culpa, no sé qué digo! –grita el estudiante.

–¡Ay del ladrón! –dice Rincón–. ¡Cómo se le ocurre robar el dinero de la Iglesia! Pero –digo yo, por hablar de otra cosa– ¿cuánto gana al año *vuestra merced* con ese trabajo?

–¡Y yo qué sé! –grita el estudiante muy enfadado–. Estoy cansado de hablar y sólo quiero encontrar mi bolsa. Si *vos* sabéis donde está, bien, y si no, me voy a buscarla ahora mismo.

Hace calor. El estudiante está muy nervioso y se limpia la cara con un pañuelo muy bonito y bastante caro. Cortado lo sigue deprisa por la plaza y, cuando el estudiante no se da cuenta, le roba también el pañuelo.

IV

Un joven que ha visto todo lo que ha pasado, llama a Rincón y a Cortado.

–Señores, ¿por casualidad son *vuestras mercedes* amigos del dinero de los demás?

–Perdónenos, caballero, pero no entendemos su pregunta –contesta Rincón.

–Entonces voy a hablarles más claro. Pregunto, señores, si *vuestras mercedes* son ladrones. Pero no sé para qué les pregunto esto. Ya sé que lo son. Pero, díganme, ¿por qué no han pagado al señor Monipodio?

–Pero bueno, ¿es que en esta ciudad hay que pagar para ser ladrón? –pregunta Cortado enfadado.

–¡Caballero! si *vuestras mercedes* no pagan, deben al menos presentarse a nuestro jefe, el señor Monipodio. Él tiene que saber quiénes son, de dónde vienen, en qué trabajan... Y si no lo hacen así, van a tener serios problemas –explica el chico.

–Está bien, señor. Si así lo hacen los ladrones en Sevilla, así debemos hacer nosotros. Pero yo siempre he pensado que robar es una profesión libre. Sí, yo creo que no hay que pagar a nadie para hacer este trabajo. Pero no quiero hablar más. Vamos a ver al señor Monipodio, que debe ser un hombre muy amable, además de bueno en su trabajo –decide Cortado.

–¡Ya lo creo! –dice el chico.

–¿Por casualidad es *vuestra merced* ladrón? –le pregunta Cortado.

–Sí señor. Yo también soy ladrón para servir a Dios[18] y a la buena gente.

–¿Un ladrón que sirve a Dios y a las buenas gentes? ¡Qué cosa más rara!

–Señor –contesta el chico–, yo pienso que cada uno en su profesión puede servir a Dios. Ya lo dice el señor Monipodio: «Después de robar, debéis dar siempre algún dinero a la Iglesia». Además, nosotros rezamos[19] todos los días, no robamos los viernes... Ah, y tampoco hablamos con mujeres llamadas María los sábados.

–Pero, con esa vida de ladrón, ¿cree de verdad *vuestra merced* que puede ir al cielo? –pregunta Cortado.

–Claro, señor. Ser ladrón no es tan malo. Es peor no creer en Dios o matar al padre o a la madre o...

–Todo está mal –dice Cortado–. Pero, bueno, ya hemos hablado bastante. Dese prisa, caballero, porque yo ya tengo ganas de saludar al señor Monipodio.

–Muy pronto va a poder verlo. Estamos ya delante de sus casa. Espérenme *vuestras mercedes* en la puerta. Yo voy a entrar antes para ver si está ocupado.

El joven entra en una casa sucia y fea. Pocos minutos más tarde, abre otra vez la puerta y llama a Rincón y Cortado.

–*Vuestras mercedes* pueden pasar. Esperen aquí, en el patio[20]. Don Monipodio los va a recibir en seguida.

Rincón y Cortado entran en un patio muy limpio, con una planta en el medio y sillas alrededor. Cerca del patio hay una pequeña habitación con un cuadro de Nuestra Señora de las Aguas[21] en la pared.

De pronto empieza a llegar mucha gente. Primero entran dos estudiantes. Luego unos chicos con sus cestas y varios hombres altos y fuertes que llevan espada. Todos ellos se pasean por el patio. Poco después llega una vieja que, sin decir nada, entra a rezar en la habitación de la Virgen[22]. En pocos minutos han entrado en el patio once o doce personas.

V

En aquel momento Monipodio baja la escalera. Todos callan y bajan la cabeza. Luego, uno a uno, le dan un beso en la mano. Más que un ladrón, Monipodio parece un rey.

Monipodio es un hombre de cuarenta y cinco o cuarenta y seis años, alto, fuerte y muy moreno. Viste pantalón ancho, camisa abierta y capa que le llega hasta los pies. Usa sombrero y lleva una espada muy pequeña.

Monipodio baja con Ganchuelo, el chico que ha traído hasta aquí a Cortado y a Rincón. Ganchuelo les presenta a su jefe:

–Éstos son los chicos que encontré esta mañana. He hablado bastante con ellos y creo que pueden trabajar con nosotros.

–Bien, bien, chicos –dice Monipodio–. ¿Cuál es vuestra profesión? ¿De dónde sois? ¿Quiénes son vuestros padres?

–¡Cuántas preguntas hace *vuestra merced*! –dice Rincón–. Caballero, nuestra vida no interesa a nadie y tampoco interesa el nombre de nuestros padres. Porque luego,

Monipodio es un hombre de cuarenta y cinco o cuarenta y seis años, alto, fuerte y muy moreno.

si nuestra suerte es mala, no queremos meter en problemas a nuestras familias. Nosotros sólo queremos trabajar en esta ciudad y por eso estamos aquí.

–Decís bien, joven, pero al menos debo saber vuestros nombres.

–Yo me llamo Rincón y mi amigo se llama Cortado.

–Pues yo os voy a llamar a *vos*, Rincón, Rinconete, y a *vos*, Cortado, Cortadillo... En esta cofradía[23] nos gusta saber quiénes son los padres de todos los que trabajan con nosotros. Y es que, una vez al año, rezamos todos juntos por los parientes que han muerto. Ese mismo día, rezamos también por todos nuestros amigos: el guardia que nos avisa del peligro, el corregidor que olvida nuestros asuntos...

De repente, Monipodio se calla y pregunta a Ganchuelo:

–¿Están los vigilantes[24] en su sitio?

–Sí, claro, –contesta el chico–. Tenemos a tres hombres en la calle. No debemos preocuparnos.

–Muy bien. Entonces podemos hablar tranquilos –dice Monipodio–. Decidme, chicos, ¿qué sabéis hacer?

–Yo, señor –dice Rinconete–, sé preparar las cartas y, así, gano siempre en el juego.

–Hombre –contesta Monipodio–, eso está bien. Preparar las cartas es buena cosa. Pero eso lo hace todo el mundo, hasta las personas que empiezan en la profesión.

Debéis estudiar nuevos trucos. Pero no os preocupéis. Yo os voy a dar muchos buenos consejos. Y *vos*, Cortadillo, ¿qué sabéis hacer?

–Señor, yo sé el truco de «meter dos y sacar veinte»: meto las dos manos en la bolsa de un señor, y saco veinte escudos de oro. ¡Y soy muy rápido en mi trabajo!

–¿Y qué otras cosas hacéis? –pregunta otra vez Monipodio.

–Lo siento, señor, pero no sé hacer más trabajos.

–Tranquilo, Cortadillo –contesta Monipodio–, porque estáis en la mejor escuela del mundo. Yo os voy a enseñar alguna cosa más. Bien, chicos, ya sabéis que en nuestra profesión hay que tener siempre la boca cerrada, ¿verdad?

–¡Pues claro, señor Monipodio! –dice Cortado–. No somos tontos. Nosotros vemos, oímos y callamos.

–Entonces, no es necesario hablar más –decide Monipodio–. Creo que sois dos buenas personas y eso es bastante. Ahora mismo vais a entrar en nuestra cofradía.

–¡Muy bien! –grita la gente que está en el patio.

VI

U<small>N</small> chico llega muy asustado a la casa.

–¡Viene el alguacil[25]! –grita–. Pero no trae a los guardias...

–Tranquilos todos –dice Monipodio–. El alguacil es amigo mío. Voy a hablar con él.

Monipodio sale a la puerta de su casa. Al poco tiempo vuelve a entrar y pregunta en voz alta:

–¿Alguno de vosotros ha trabajado hoy en la plaza de San Salvador?

–Sí, yo estuve allí, señor –contesta Ganchuelo.

–Entonces, ¿por qué no me habéis enseñado la bolsa de color amarillo que se perdió en la plaza?

–¡Es que yo no he robado esa bolsa, señor! ¡Y tampoco sé quién lo hizo! –dice Ganchuelo.

–Pues tenemos que encontrar esa bolsa. Lo pide el alguacil, que es amigo mío. Este hombre me hace muchos favores al año.

Ganchuelo dice una y otra vez que él no sabe nada. Monipodio se enfada cada vez más y grita:

–¡De mí no se ríe nadie! ¡Vamos! ¿Dónde está esa bolsa?

En ese momento, Rinconete comprende que el asunto es serio. Pide consejo a su amigo Cortadillo y saca de entre su ropa la bolsa de color amarillo.

–Se acabó el problema. Ésta es la bolsa que pide el alguacil. Mi amigo Cortadillo se la robó a un estudiante esta mañana. Aquí está todo: la bolsa, los quince escudos de oro que tenía dentro y el pañuelo del estudiante.

–¡Ay, ay, Cortadillo el Bueno! –dice sonriendo Monipodio–. Así os voy a llamar desde ahora. Escuchad: el pañuelo es para *vos* y la bolsa para el alguacil, porque el estudiante es pariente suyo. Ya sabéis, debemos tener siempre contentos a los guardias...

VII

Monipodio sale a la calle para darle la bolsa al alguacil. A los pocos minutos vuelve con dos mujeres. Éstas llevan vestidos muy escotados[26] y la boca pintada de rojo. Las mujeres ríen y hablan con dos de los hombres que están en el patio: Chiquiznaque y Maniferro. Rinconete y Cortadillo se dan cuenta en seguida de que son dos prostitutas[27]. Detrás de ellas viene un chico, que deja una cesta muy grande en el suelo. Todos se ponen muy contentos. La Escalanta y la Gananciosa –pues así se llaman las chicas– han traído la comida.

En ese momento sale al patio la vieja que estaba en la habitación de la Virgen. Esta mujer, la señora Pipota, habla con Monipodio.

–Ayer el Renegado y el Centopiés dejaron una cesta de ropa en mi casa. No contaron las chaquetas y los pantalones que había en ella, pero yo –bien lo sabe Dios– no he cogido nada. En mi casa tengo la cesta robada.

–Bueno, señora Pipota –dice Monipodio–. Esta misma noche puedo ir a su casa.

–Entonces me voy –dice la vieja–. Tengo que comprar unas flores a Nuestra Señora de las Aguas y ya es tarde. Pero me duele mucho la cabeza... Por favor, Escalanta, ¿tienes un poco de vino para esta vieja? Sólo un vasito. Un poquito de vino es lo mejor para mi pobre cabeza.

–Aquí lo tiene, señora Pipota –dice la Escalanta– y le da un gran vaso de vino a la vieja.

–Gracias Escalanta, es que no he desayunado, ¿sabes? Bueno, me voy. Eh, niñas, ¿tenéis un poco de dinero? Es que, con las prisas, olvidé mi bolso en casa y no traigo dinero para las flores.

–Yo tengo dinero, señora Pipota –dice la Gananciosa.

–Y yo también –contesta la Escalanta.

La vieja coge deprisa el dinero de las chicas y les dice adiós a todos:

–¡A divertirse y a vivir tranquilos! Ahora sois jóvenes y tenéis toda la vida por delante. Y, sobre todo, no os preocupéis por los guardias. Dios siempre ayuda a la buena gente.

VIII

LA vieja se ha ido. Monipodio y su gente, con el cuchillo en la mano, se sientan alrededor de la cesta. Es la hora de comer y tienen mucha hambre. La Gananciosa saca más de tres kilos de naranjas, luego un plato grande con trozos de pescado, medio queso de Flandes[28], aceitunas, pan y vino.

De repente, alguien llama a la puerta y todos se asustan. Todos menos Monipodio que, muy tranquilo, pregunta:

–¿Quién llama?

–Soy Tagarete, el vigilante. Aquí viene Juliana la Cariharta. Está llorando a gritos, porque algo malo le ha pasado.

Monipodio, tranquilo como siempre, abre la puerta y entra la Cariharta. La mujer parece de la misma profesión que las otras dos.

–¡Pido ayuda a Dios contra ese ladrón, contra ese mal hombre que me ha robado los mejores años de mi vida! ¡Casi me mata!

–Tranquila, Cariharta –dice Monipodio–. Aquí estoy yo para ayudarte. Vamos, vamos, ¿qué pasa? ¿Te has enfadado con tu protector[29]?

–¿Mi protector? –grita la Cariharta–. ¡Mire *vuestra merced*! ¡Así me paga mi protector!

Juliana se levanta las faldas y enseña sus piernas llenas de cardenales[30].

–El Repolido me ha pegado[31] –explica Juliana–. Él estaba jugando a las cartas. Perdía y me mandó a buscar treinta reales para pagar en el juego. Yo le traje sólo veinticuatro, porque no conseguí más. Pero el Repolido se pensó que yo me guardaba seis reales. Como es un animal, esta mañana me llevó al campo y allí casi me mata. ¡Por eso pido ayuda contra ese mal hombre!

–Juliana –dice la Gananciosa–, ya sabes que «el que bien te quiere te hace llorar». Vamos a ver, después de pegarte, ¿no te dio un beso el Repolido?

–Un beso sólo no. Me dio mil besos –contesta la Cariharta–. Y hasta lloraba por haberme pegado.

–¿Lo ves? –dice la Gananciosa–. Seguro que viene en seguida a buscarte.

–¡Un momento! –grita Monipodio–. El Repolido no va a entrar en esta casa, si antes no pide perdón a la Cariharta. ¡Vamos, hombre! ¡Hay que ser mala persona para hacer una cosa así! ¡Pegar a una mujer tan limpia y buena como Juliana...!

El Repolido me ha pegado...
¡Por eso pido ayuda contra ese mal hombre!

–¡Ay, por Dios! –grita la Cariharta–. Cállese *vuestra merced*. No quiero oír esas palabras. Ay, don Monipodio, ahora me acuerdo del Repolido... ¡Y creo que lo quiero más que antes! Tengo ganas de ir a buscarlo.

–No debes hacer eso, Juliana, porque en otra ocasión el Repolido puede pegarte mucho más. Quédate aquí –dice la Gananciosa–. Y, si el Repolido no viene a buscarte, no te preocupes. Le vamos a mandar una cartita que le va a dejar las cosas muy claras.

–¡Eso sí! –contesta la Cariharta–, porque tengo mil cosas que escribirle.

–Muy bien –dice Monipodio–, pero ahora debemos seguir con la comida.

IX

Dos viejos de la cofradía preguntan a Monipodio si pueden volver a su trabajo.

–Podéis ir tranquilos –contesta éste–, pero debéis volver pronto con toda la información necesaria.

–¿Quiénes son esos dos? –pregunta Rinconete.

–¡Oh! Son dos caballeros muy buenos que trabajan para nosotros. Durante el día pasean por toda la ciudad y eligen las casas que nosotros podemos robar más tarde, por la noche. Además, nos avisan siempre que alguien va por la calle con la bolsa bien llena de dinerito.

De repente, alguien llama a la puerta.

–¿Quién es? –pregunta Monipodio.

–Soy yo, el Repolido. Por favor, ¿me deja pasar *vuestra merced*?

–¡No, señor Monipodio! –grita la Cariharta–. ¡Aquí no debe entrar ese mal hombre!

Monipodio no escucha a Juliana y abre la puerta. La chica corre a la habitación de la Virgen y cierra con llave por dentro.

El Repolido entra en la casa y llama a la Cariharta.

–Cariharta, mujer, no te enfades conmigo por más tiempo.

–Déjame tranquila, mal hombre. No quiero verte nunca más.

–Vamos, sal de ahí y vuelve a casa conmigo. Debemos olvidarlo todo...

–¡Fuera de aquí, Repolido! –grita la Cariharta.

El Repolido se enfada.

–Cariharta, me estoy cansando de esperar. ¡Abre la puerta de una vez! Si no lo haces, lo vas a pasar muy mal...

–¡Caballero! –grita Monipodio–. Nadie habla así en mi casa. Cariharta está asustada y no quiere veros. Dejadme a mí. Voy a hablar yo con ella.

Monipodio se acerca a la puerta y llama a Cariharta.

–¡Ah, Juliana! ¡Ah, niña! ¡Cariharta mía! Sal fuera, por favor. El Repolido te va a pedir perdón, ¿verdad?

–Bueno... –dice el Repolido–. Pedir perdón no es cosa fácil para un hombre como yo. Pero, si Juliana quiere, yo le pido perdón una y mil veces.

Chiquiznaque y Maniferro se ríen de las palabras del Repolido y éste se enfada muchísimo:

–¿Quién se está riendo de mí? Andaos con cuidado. Por asuntos más pequeños, he matado ya a más de un hombre...

–*Vos* también debéis tener cuidado, Repolido, porque no me gustan estas bromas –contesta enfadado Chiquiznaque.

Los tres hombres se preparan para pelear. Por suerte, en ese momento, la Cariharta, que ha oído los gritos, sale de la habitación. La chica se acerca al Repolido, le coge de la capa y le da un beso.

–No pelees más, vida de mi vida, luz de mis ojos –le dice Juliana al Repolido–. Ahora mismo nos vamos tú y yo a casa juntitos.

–Los amigos no deben pelear entre sí ni enfadarse unos con otros –dice Monipodio–. Debéis daros todos la mano y quedar como amigos.

El Repolido y Chiquiznaque se dan la mano. La Escalanta empieza entonces a cantar:

Por un sevillano duro y frío
tengo el corazón herido.

Y sigue así la Gananciosa:

Por un hombre moreno de color verde
quién es la mujer que no se pierde.

La Cariharta no quiere ser menos:

Párate, enfadado, no me pegues más
que, si bien lo miras, a tus carnes das.

Chiquiznaque va a empezar otra canción cuando, de repente, vuelven a llamar a la puerta. Monipodio sale a ver qué ocurre.

–¡El Corregidor va a pasar ahora mismo por esta calle! –grita el vigilante.

Todos se quedan callados. La fiesta se ha acabado. La gente de Monipodio, muerta de miedo, empieza a correr hacia el piso de arriba. El patio se queda en silencio. Todos se han ido. Bueno, todos no. Rinconete y Cortadillo siguen allí, sentados sin saber qué hacer.

Pocos minutos más tarde, vuelve el vigilante y grita:

–¡Pueden salir! ¡Ya se ha ido el Corregidor!

X

No se ha ido todavía el vigilante cuando llega a la casa de Monipodio un hombre con la cara muy seria. Monipodio le manda pasar y llama a Chiquiznaque, a Maniferro y al Repolido.

–¿Qué le pasa *a vuestra merced*? –pregunta Monipodio–. Parece estar muy enfadado.

–Lo estoy, señor Monipodio, lo estoy. Vamos a ver, hace unos días yo le mandé dar una cuchillada[32] de catorce puntos[33] al caballero de la esquina, y *vuestra merced* no lo ha hecho. ¿Puedo saber por qué?

Monipodio pregunta a Chiquiznaque:

–¿Qué ha ocurrido con ese trabajo?

–Ayer estuve esperando a ese caballero en la puerta de su casa. Pero, cuando llegó a su portal, vi que su cara era muy pequeña. Yo no podía dar una cuchillada de catorce puntos en una cara así... ¡No había sitio, señor Monipodio!

–Bueno, bueno. Entonces ¿qué hicisteis?

–¡Hombre! –explica Chiquiznaque–, el trabajo lo tenía que hacer... Y no vi otra solución que darle la cuchillada de catorce puntos al criado[34] del caballero. ¡Ése sí tenía la cara grande!

–Pero, ¡por Dios! –grita el hombre–, era mejor dar una cuchillada de siete puntos al caballero, que una de catorce a su criado. Ya veo que he perdido los treinta escudos que le pagué. Por suerte, no es demasiado dinero... Bueno, caballeros, tengo prisa. Adiós. Yo ya me voy.

–¡Ah, no! –dice Monipodio–. Eso no es así. Señor, nosotros hemos hecho nuestro trabajo. El precio era de cincuenta escudos y *vuestra merced* ha pagado sólo treinta. Nos debe veinte escudos.

–Pero ¿cómo voy a pagar por un trabajo que no está bien hecho? Yo mando dar una cuchillada al caballero y *vuestra merced* ¡se la da a su criado!

–Eso da igual, señor –explica Chiquiznaque–. Mi abuelo siempre decía: «Quien mal quiere a Torcuato, mal quiere a su gato». Torcuato es el caballero; *vuestra merced* no lo quiere. El criado es el gato. Pues bien, si le pego al gato, también le pego a Torcuato. ¿Entiende, señor? El caballero y el gato son una misma cosa. Por eso, el asunto está muy claro: *vuestra merced* debe pagar los veinte escudos que debe al señor Monipodio.

–¡Habláis bien, Chiquiznaque! Y a *vuestra merced* –dice Monipodio– no pienso repetírselo más veces: primero debe pagarme el dinero que nos debe. Y luego, si todavía piensa como antes, el caballero de la esquina puede recibir una cuchillada.

—Sí —contesta el caballero—. Eso es lo que quiero. Además, voy a pagar ahora mismo. Aquí le dejo estas joyas de oro. Son para pagar los veinte escudos que debo y los cuarenta escudos que son el precio de este nuevo trabajo.

Monipodio coge las joyas y las mira una y otra vez. Cuando ve que de verdad son de oro, las guarda deprisa en su bolsa.

—Bien, caballero —dice sonriendo—. Esta misma noche, el caballero de la esquina va a recibir una bonita cuchillada. Os doy palabra de Monipodio.

—Eso espero. Adiós.

Rinconete empieza otra vez a leer. Todos lo escuchan en silencio.

XI

Monipodio llama a toda su gente y abre un libro. Como no sabe leer, pide ayuda a Rinconete. El joven empieza a leer en voz alta:

Trabajos que debemos hacer esta semana

Primero: cuchilladas

–La primera, al caballero de la esquina: vale cincuenta escudos. Hemos recibido treinta. El trabajo lo va a hacer Chiquiznaque.

–Me parece que esta semana no había más cuchilladas –dice Monipodio–. Leed el punto sobre «golpes».

Rinconete empieza otra vez a leer. Todos lo escuchan en silencio.

Segundo: golpes

–Doce golpes fuertes al hombre de la tienda de la plaza. El precio es de un escudo por golpe. Ya hemos dado ocho golpes. Los otros cuatro debe darlos Maniferro esta semana.

–Ese trabajo está hecho. ¿Hay más golpes, hijo?

–Sí, señor, uno más –responde el chico.

–*Seis golpes para el hombre llamado Silguero. El precio es de seis escudos. El trabajo lo va a hacer el Repolido.*

–¿Todavía hay más, joven?

–Sí, señor. El libro sigue aún durante un buen rato.

–Pues dejadlo ya, porque se está haciendo tarde y hace mucho calor –dice Monipodio–. Ahora, volved todos a vuestro sitio. El domingo que viene os espero aquí en mi casa. Como siempre, debéis traer todas las cosas robadas durante la semana. ¡Y he dicho todas! Ya sabéis que yo luego os doy vuestra parte del dinero. ¡Ah! Rinconete y Cortadillo trabajan esta semana en las calles que están cerca del río. *Vos*, Ganchoso, vais con ellos y les enseñáis dónde pueden trabajar. El río es un buen sitio. He visto a otros menos listos que ellos sacar de allí mucho dinero.

Monipodio saca un papel en blanco y le dice así a Rinconete:

–Escribid aquí vuestro nombre y el de Cortadillo. Debéis decir así: «En el día de hoy, entran en la cofradía de Monipodio Rinconete y Cortadillo. Rinconete: trucos de cartas. Cortadillo: ladrón de bolsas». Si así lo queréis, podéis callar el nombre de vuestros padres y el pueblo del que venís.

Poco a poco, el patio de Monipodio se está quedando vacío. Ya se han ido Repolido y la Cariharta, la Escalanta y Maniferro, la Gananciosa y Chiquiznaque... Después de dar un beso en la mano a Monipodio, se van también Rinconete y Cortadillo.

Rinconete y Cortadillo piensan en todo lo que han visto y oído este día. Rinconete es muy joven, pero es un chico listo y muy bueno en el fondo. Sabe leer y escribir. Su padre –aquel hombre tan importante que vendía bulas para la Iglesia– le enseñó cuando era niño. Él entiende qué cosas son buenas y qué otras no lo son.

La cofradía de Monipodio le parece muy original. ¡Todos usan unas palabras tan divertidas! ¡Y ese señor Monipodio, que parece un rey más que un ladrón! Y lo más extraño: todos ellos son ladrones, hombres que viven de la mentira; y, sin embargo, piensan que Dios los ayuda y que, con la vida que llevan, pueden ganar el cielo.

Pero Rinconete sabe que se equivocan. Sabe que a Dios no puede gustarle esa vida. Y no sólo eso. Una ciudad tan grande, tan rica y famosa como Sevilla no puede estar así, en manos de tanta mala gente.

No, los dos chicos no pueden seguir mucho tiempo en esta cofradía. Rinconete debe proponerle a su amigo cambiar de profesión y dejar esa vida demasiado libre y llena de peligros.

Pero Rinconete y Cortadillo son aún muy jóvenes y no quieren preocuparse. Todavía van a pasar unos meses en la cofradía del señor Monipodio... Unos meses llenos de aventuras que os tengo que contar en otro libro.

SOBRE LA LECTURA

Para comprobar la comprensión

I

1. *¿En qué trabajan los padres de Rincón y Cortado?*
2. *¿Qué hacía Rincón con el dinero de la Iglesia cuando trabajaba con su padre?*
3. *El Corregidor de Toledo quiso conocer a Cortado. ¿Por qué?*

II

4. *¿Por qué se enfada el viajero con los chicos?*
5. *¿Hacia dónde van los caballeros?*
6. *¿Qué roba Cortado al final del viaje? ¿Qué hace con las cosas que ha robado?*
7. *¿Qué trabajo van a hacer los dos jóvenes en Sevilla?*

III

8. *¿Qué roba Cortado al estudiante?*
9. *¿Por qué se enfada el estudiante con Cortado?*

IV

10. *¿Por qué deben ir los chicos a casa de Monipodio?*
11. *¿Cómo sirve a Dios la gente de Monipodio?*
12. *¿Qué ocurre mientras los dos amigos esperan en el patio?*

V

13. *¿Cómo saluda a Monipodio la gente del patio?*
14. *¿Cómo va a llamar Monipodio a Rincón y Cortado?*
15. *¿Qué piensa Monipodio de los trucos de los chicos?*

VI

16. *¿Por qué se enfada Monipodio con Ganchuelo?*
17. *¿Por qué es importante encontrar la bolsa del estudiante? ¿Quién tiene la bolsa?*
18. *¿Qué hace Cortadillo?*

VII

19. *¿Quiénes son las dos mujeres que entran con Monipodio? ¿Qué traen a casa de Monipodio?*
20. *¿Qué tiene en su casa la señora Pipota? ¿Roba ella también?*
21. *¿Qué dos cosas pide la señora Pipota a las chicas?*

VIII

22. *¿Por qué Juliana va a casa de Monipodio? ¿Por qué la ha pegado el Repolido?*

IX

23. *¿Por qué quieren pelearse el Repolido, Chiquiznaque y Maniferro?*
24. *¿Se pelean al final? ¿Por qué?*

X

25. *¿Por qué no dio Chiquiznaque la cuchillada al caballero? ¿A quién le dio la cuchillada?*

26. *¿Qué quiere decir, según Chiquiznaque, la expresión «Quién mal quiere a Torcuato, mal quiere a su gato»?*

XI

27. *¿Qué lee Rinconete?*

28. *¿Dónde van a trabajar Rinconete y Cortadillo?*

29. *¿Qué piensa Rinconete de la gente de Monipodio y de esa clase de vida?*

Para hablar en clase

1. **Rinconete y Cortadillo** *es una de las* **Novelas «ejemplares»** *de Cervantes: ¿Cree que su autor quiere realmente que aprendamos una lección moral?*

2. *Los personajes tienen una doble moral: por una parte son ladrones y viven de mentiras; sin embargo, son gente muy religiosa. ¿Conoce otros ejemplos de este tipo de personas?*

3. *¿Cree usted que el mundo de Rinconete y Cortadillo se parece algo al nuestro? ¿Por qué?*

NOTAS

Estas notas proponen equivalencias o explicaciones que no pretenden agotar el significado de las palabras o expresiones siguientes sino aclararlas en el contexto de *Rinconete y Cortadillo*.

m.: masculino, *f.:* femenino, *inf.:* infinitivo.

capa

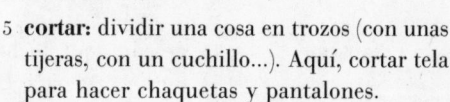

1 **venta** *f.:* lugar donde antiguamente se podía dormir y comer. Las ventas estaban situadas en medio del campo, cerca de los caminos por donde pasaban los viajeros.

2 **capa** *f.:* prenda de vestir larga y suelta, sin mangas y abierta por delante, que se lleva encima de la ropa a modo de abrigo.

3 **espada** *f.:* arma blanca de hoja de acero larga y recta.

4 **caballero** *m.:* en la Edad Media «caballero» era el noble que, en la guerra, peleaba a caballo. En el siglo XVI se usaba esta palabra para designar o dirigirse cortésmente a un señor.

5 **cortar:** dividir una cosa en trozos (con unas tijeras, con un cuchillo...). Aquí, cortar tela para hacer chaquetas y pantalones.

6 **sastre** *m.:* persona que hace trajes para hombre.

7 **bulas** *f.:* dinero que se pagaba a la Iglesia para no tener que seguir ciertas prohibiciones, tales como el «ayuno» (la Iglesia prohibía comer cualquier alimento ciertos

espada

cartas

pelear

cesta

días del año) o la «vigilia» (prohibición de comer carne en fechas concretas).

8 **reales** *m.:* monedas antiguas de muy poco valor.

9 **cartas** *f.:* con ellas jugamos al póquer, al bridge y a muchos otros juegos de mesa.

10 **la veintiuna:** juego de cartas muy popular en los siglos XVI y XVII. En él ganaba la persona que antes conseguía veintiún puntos.

11 **bolsas** *f.:* aquí, son los saquitos donde los hombres guardaban y llevaban el dinero.

12 **corregidor** *m.:* magistrado que, en nombre del rey, administraba justicia en una ciudad.

13 **trucos** *m.:* técnicas para engañar a los demás.

14 **trampas** *f.:* engaños que se hacen en el juego para ganar a los demás.

15 **pelear:** aquí, luchar dos personas e intentar hacerse daño con armas o con las manos. También se puede pelear sólo con palabras.

16 **cesta** *f.:* recipiente hecho de mimbre o cualquier otra fibra vegetal y que sirve para llevar ropas, frutas y otras cosas.

17 **escudo** *m.:* antigua moneda.

rezar

18 **servir a Dios:** adorar a Dios y seguir sus mandamientos.

19 **rezamos** (*inf.:* **rezar**): pronunciamos oraciones dirigidas a Dios o a los santos.

20 **patio** *m.:* espacio abierto o con techo de cristal, dentro de una casa. Las casas con patio son muy típicas en España, sobre todo en Andalucía.

21 **Nuestra Señora de las Aguas** *f.:* Nuestra Señora es la Virgen María, madre de Jesucristo. En los países católicos muy devotos de la Virgen, ésta recibe muchos nombres distintos y es tradicional rendir culto a «una» Virgen en particular, según las regiones, pueblos e incluso barrios.

22 **Virgen** *f.:* ver nota anterior.

23 **cofradía** *f.:* originalmente, grupo de personas que se reúnen por asuntos religiosos (por ejemplo, para rezar a la Virgen o a algún santo). En la lengua de los ladrones se refiere a una organización de personas que se asocian para realizar malas acciones.

24 **vigilantes** *m.:* aquí, personas que se ocupan de avisar de los peligros.

25 **alguacil** *m.:* empleado del corregidor.

26 **vestidos escotados** *m.:* vestidos que dejan ver parte del pecho.

27 **prostituta** *f.:* mujer «de mala vida», que vende su cuerpo a los hombres.

vestido escotado

pegar

28 **Flandes:** nombre dado a los territorios que comprendían los actuales reinos de Holanda y Bélgica, y parte de Francia.

29 **protector** *m.:* persona que protege. Aquí, se llama «protector» al hombre que vive del dinero ganado por una prostituta.

30 **cardenales** *m.:* manchas moradas que aparecen en la piel como resultado de un choque violento contra algo, un golpe, una caída, etc.

31 **me ha pegado** (*inf.:* **pegar**): me ha maltratado, me ha dado golpes fuertes.

32 **dar una cuchillada:** cortar a alguien con un cuchillo. «Cuchillada» es el golpe que se da con el cuchillo y también la herida que resulta del golpe.

cuchillada
de catorce
puntos

33 **cuchillada de catorce puntos** *f.:* el médico debe dar catorce puntos para coser o cerrar la cuchillada.

34 **criado** *m.:* hombre que trabaja en casa de otras personas y recibe por ello dinero, comida y cama.